And then I met Elvis...

DOUG BARI

Published by Doug Bari
ISBN: 978-1-985693-45-6

Cover design by Lieu Pham, Covertopia.com
Ebook formatting by Guido Henkel

Glen Cove, Maine 1969

My mother had fucked me over again. She'd stiffed yet another in a long line of landlords out of months of rent. Another move in the middle of the night. Christ, I hated her.

The moving team backed our plain white 70-foot house trailer with faux black shutters into position between two much grander mobile homes. It was obvious ours was second, maybe even third-hand. Most of the other homes had skirting around the bottoms. I knew ours wouldn't. Our wheels and whatever shit we wanted to throw under our trailer would be visible for all to see. I was already embarrassed.

Our new un-introduced neighbors came out to gawk. A couple of them lit up cigarettes and silently judged. Even in trailer parks, there are class systems.

I was 13. I'd be 14 in August.

Auburn red hair. Freckles. Skinny. Crooked teeth.

Oh, and it was the end of May. I was going to be enrolled in a new school for all of 2 weeks before the summer recess began.

My mother went down the tubes beginning in her 30s after a married man she was having an affair with dumped her. That event coincided with the death of my long gone father. Overnight, she became a drunken pirate ensconced in a lawn chair in front of the TV. My mother typically drank cheap beer, but sometimes, inferior hard liquor made its way into the picture. I'd seen her quaff cooking vanilla over ice in a pinch, but vodka was her preference. It was so rotgut, I knew even as a kid not to touch it.

My mother celebrated our successful move that night. Not like she ever needed a reason to celebrate. She regaled me with repeated and often revised tales of her bad upbringing and crowned each telling with a belt of booze and the happy admonition, "Don't point any fingers at me. I *deserve* to drink. I have a *right* to drink."

My mother was a reverent television addict, so that meant after a move, her only concern was making sure the TV still worked. For her, it was a substitution for human interaction. The boob tube came on first thing and didn't get turned off until she went to bed. She was big on medical and cop series that bored the shit out of me. No one could talk except during the commercials. She had to have the volume up to hear every nuance. If I was trying to have some kind of moment with her, she'd look past me at the TV screen, alert on something she found fascinating, and have me turn it up a few more decibels. The big ignore. Everything had to be at arm's length with her.

I'd just finished getting her another Black Label beer and a half-eaten piece of blueberry pie. When I gave her the pie, she pulled the plate close and hovered over it protectively. Jesus. Like I was going to steal her fuckin' pie. God.

I tried to slink off to my room without making eye contact.

No such luck. I had a steady job as the remote control.

"Timmy, I need you to change the channel," she commanded through her pie-hole filled with mashed up pie.

Dammit.

I eye-rolled back into the room and robotically turned the dial.

"What channel?"

"I just don't want to watch any bullshit *Gentle Ben* stories with a goddam bear."

I stopped on *Land of the Giants*.

"Oh, God no," she cried as if I'd stabbed her with a hot poker.

"I thought you knew what you wanted to see."

"Just don't go by too fast—" she choked. Bits of pie sprayed out.

She was flustered which was always funny shit when she got that jacked up. Her face turned purple as she struggled for air. She grabbed her drink and wolfed vodka in an effort to clear her throat. She tried to sit up from her slumped position, but couldn't. Her heavy ass was wedged in the back of the chair. "Don't—god*dammit*—do what I *tell* you, goddammit!"

I stopped on channel 13. CBS. *The Wild Wild West* was in its last act. She fretted, but hesitated about passing to another channel because she knew *Gomer Pyle U.S.M.C.* was coming on right after. She liked Gomer and so did I—one of the few things we agreed on. If she followed her normal pattern, she'd stay awake through Private Pyle, then make a charade of watching the *CBS Friday Night Movie*, only to fall asleep ten minutes into it and wake groggily when the end credits were almost done rolling.

She made me stand there forever.

"Stay or not?" I asked. "You want to go back to the bear?"

She got all twitchy like she was going to shit herself—flailing away in her recliner. "Oh…oh…oh…Jesus-Mary-mother-of-God…oh, alright." Then she settled as quickly as she'd gone into orbit. Whatever bug she had up her ass was dead. She pointed to the TV. "Leave it there."

She invited me to stay. She must have been really lonely. "You can watch TV if you don't talk."

It was too early to go to bed. I opted to be the obedient pussy so I could watch something—*anything*—to pass the time. I understood the escape television provided. I used it extensively. It kept my sanity on many a night.

I sat on the floor in front of the TV and did my best to concentrate on Jim and Artemis while my mother hurled barbs over my shoulder.

My mother felt free to break her own rule and talk during TV episodes I was watching. Everybody needs a drunk critic in the room when they're trying to watch *The Wild Wild West*.

"I don't like this Jim West character. He's too much—look how tight his pants are. You can tell he's in love with himself. He thinks his shit doesn't stink. People like that think they shit ice cream."

She fancied herself quite the clever comedian. I just wanted her to shut up with her narrow-minded opinions.

During a commercial, I heard my mother snoring. Man. She hadn't even made it to Gomer. She was outdoing herself. She must have been extra tired from moving in.

I studied her head tilted over to one side as if her neck had been broken. Mouth hanging open half-way. Sawing logs.

At least she hadn't asked for the bucket.

The Puke Bucket

If I thought I was depressed on Friday when we moved in, I wasn't really. The black hole I fell into over the weekend took me to the true depths of depression. I was fucked.

The roads through the rustic wooded park were a mix of dirt and gravel that kicked up dust. It was a two-minute walk from my front door to the entrance where the dilapidated *Sunshine Acres Mobile Home Park* sign hung crookedly off to one side. Directly across the street from the entrance was the school bus stop.

Glen Cove had a fair amount of homes along its streets, but little else. It didn't take me long to figure out my geographic status. Our hidden trailer park was carved out of a swath of woods surrounded by much nicer places of abode.

Up behind the bus stop was an abandoned shell of a building that had been a truck-stop once. The faded sign read *Pupp's Good Eats.*

Facing out the entrance, if I turned left and walked a few miles, I hit a strip mall after tripping over a couple of convenience stores. If I turned right and walked not even a mile, there was an entrance to the Maine coastline. People navigated down a short path to a beach that was muddy in places, studded with rocks and broken shells. And even though the weather was sunny and relatively mild, the water was cold as hell. Ice cubes.

I'd finished taking stock of my immediate surroundings by Saturday afternoon.

My mother was in a pretty good mood that night. Laughing. Not too much weeping. She'd been into the sauce early. She made some *Jiffy Pop* popcorn and we watched television together. We even played a game of *Parcheesi*. She could get vicious when she was losing, so I was happy she won. After her victory, she faded in and out, but remained relatively docile.

At one point when she seemed pretty gone with the wind, I quietly attempted to change the channel, but she had a motion detector that brought her back to life when I got near the dial.

She sprung forward in her chair as much as she could. "I was watching that! Leave that alone!"

So I put it back. And she went right back into a coma.

Overall, it wasn't a bad night at all.

I should have known that was the setup for Sunday.

Sunday night's scenario played out like a repeat of an aberration I'd been through hundreds of times. My mother was predictable enough, even to herself. If I saw her grab her plastic puke bucket from under the kitchen sink and set it down beside her recliner before she even popped her first 16-ounce Schlitz or Black Label, I knew how the evening was going to go.

The preface to the crying drunk part of the experience was always boisterous hilarity on her part. Even if her stories were not funny, she would find an odd humor in her circumstances and laugh uproariously. The drunker, the louder.

I always knew things were going unavoidably south when she told me she loved me. My mother never told me she loved me unless she was in her cups and then it was a weeping slobbering affair that disgusted the hell out of me. In my mind, if she had to get wasted to break down enough to tell me she loved me, she might as well have never said it at all. Her emoting meant nothing to me. It was especially depressing when I could see it coming. I'd had the unfortunate benefit of seeing it coming since I was eight or nine.

She'd already performed for me. We'd been through some hilarity and a touch of sobbing "I love you, Timmy" stuff. Several times, mid-sentence, she'd reached over and opened up into the bucket. She'd finish the hurl, spit a couple of times, sit back up, and finish her thought.

By 6 PM she was full throttle into her crying phase, breaking down in between anointing herself. The next step was always the task of getting her into bed before she passed out. Extensive vomiting was a given. There was never any doubt about that. You just hoped she used the bucket or made it to the bathroom in time. It was half and half on the success rate.

By the time she got to the puking stage, she was legless. I knew if she hadn't already thrown up and she was able to get out of her chair, I'd better be right behind her with the bucket. When she was out of it, blindly feeling her way along the walls, occasionally crawling, she spewed wherever the moment of inspiration came to her. Which was okay in her mind because she knew I'd be the one cleaning it up.

Sometimes it would be one big purge, other times it came in accents. Either way, getting the bucket in line with her haphazard aim was certainly more preferable to having to go back later in the wee hours of the morning and wipe down walls. Although given the choice, wiping down a wall was much easier than trying to eradicate stinky particles of vomit out of crummy carpeting or the folds of her chair.

My mother was in her judgmental armchair critic mode which was really pissing me off, but I didn't dare say anything.

Disney's Wonderful World of Color was on, just not in color. I normally only saw the first half hour of any story because my mother adored *The Ed Sullivan Show* that began 30 minutes into Disney's hour. If Ed Sullivan had Tessie O'Shea or fuckin' Topo Gigio on, my mother was all over it. But the moment Ed brought something like The Beatles to the stage, she'd get antsy and threaten to flick the dial, even back to Disney which she didn't care for.

I saw it for the power trip it was. During times like that, if she was having me stand at the TV and turn the dial for her until she found something she liked, I could usually convince her to go back after only missing a few minutes of what I so desperately wanted to see.

Sure enough, as soon as Ed's start time rolled up, she ordered me to flip the channel dial like she was cutting off my rations. I stood up and did as I was told.

"God, why can't I ever watch the rest?"

"Stop swearing."

"I'm not swearing."

"You said 'God.'"

"That's not swearing."

"It is the way you say it."

"Well, what about you? You swear all the time."

Calling my mother out was risky. But she asked for it sometimes. Especially when it was obvious I was right.

She lowered the glasses she used to watch TV and cut me with her eyes. "I don't have to listen to your backtalk." Then she laid out my options. "Hey, you can just go to bed."

At that point, I didn't care if I went to bed or not. With or without supper. I made an attempt at a getaway, but the moment I stepped away from the set, the picture started rolling up at half-second intervals.

"Hey," she alerted. "Hit it," she instructed.

Shut up. I knew what to do. I slapped the TV on the top right of the cabinet. The picture slowed to 1-second rolls. Better. I popped it again, and this time, the picture stabilized. But then the vertical hold wavered. What the hell. A side adjustment.

"Hit it!"

"I know! You don't have to tell me!"

I cuffed the TV on its right side once and the picture straightened out.

When I stepped back from the set, the picture snowed. I adjusted the rabbit ears and tightened the crinkled aluminum foil wrapped around the ends. I held my breath. The picture held. I wiped imaginary sweat off my brow.

"There. Anything else?"

She waved me away and I retreated to my room and closed the door. I reached up in my closet and secured my handful of Forrest J Ackerman *Famous Monsters of Filmland* magazines. I lost myself in re-reading articles I'd read dozens of times.

She passed out and snored sporadically for a couple of hours.

I fell asleep on my back with a Bela Lugosi Dracula issue tented over my chest protecting me.

Around midnight, she woke me up with wounded animal gagging sounds. I went out to the living room where I found her pushing herself up out of her recliner with brownish spit hanging from one side of her mouth.

"I'm going to bed!" she announced as she wrestled to a standing position.

I grabbed the bucket by the edge that didn't have some shit running down the side and trailed behind her with nasty smelling upchuck sloshing around.

She yelled over her shoulder, "Don't spill it! Don't spill it!"

Long after I was asleep, I heard her calling my name accompanied by "Help me." I'd placed her bucket by the side of her bed where I always put it for her use during the night. In her defense, she'd rolled over in her stupor and made an attempt. Some had actually gone into the bucket, but most of it had found a home running down the outside of her mattress and box spring.

My mother seemed to be an expert at taking bad situations and hurling gasoline on the fire. Through her putrid fog, she instructed, "Go get a rag and clean it up." Like I needed her sage advice.

When I finished with puke maintenance, it was going on 4 AM. I had to get up for school and be waiting for the bus at 7:30.

I crept back into bed and hoped she'd stay blacked out.

For the longest time, I thought this kind of behavior was normal.

First Day at the New School

I dreaded Monday morning rolling around.

There didn't seem to be any kids my age in the trailer park, so I walked to the bus stop by myself.

I spotted the bad characters right away and they scoped me out just as fast.

Moosie was the ringleader. A true bully. Tiny for his age. But there were storms in this guy's eyes. You could see the darkness swirling around in his head.

He had a couple of big goons. Elwood and Richard. Elwood was a dolt and Richard was a little smarter, but not by much.

Cowering off to the side was this waif named Harry. He clearly was trying to be invisible, but bullies see right through the invisibility cloak. The weaker you are, the better the sport. I wondered what kind of inner anger motivates these fucks. Especially when their clothes and shoes dripped money and mine didn't. What'd they have to be pissed about?

One thing was clear from the get-go. No doubt about it. By all appearances, I was the fuckin' welfare kid.

Moosie flicked Harry behind the ear. It snapped so you knew it hurt. Harry flinched, but didn't react. It would be suicide to do so.

Moosie signaled to Elwood who pushed Harry off the curb into the street right as a car whizzed by, narrowly missing him.

Elwood laughed. "Hey, you better watch out, stupid."

Harry clambered back up on the sidewalk and got his footing.

Moosie swung around Harry and slapped him smartly against his right ear. Boxed it good. The poor kid couldn't help but recoil in defensive posture.

Moosie slapped Harry's left ear harder than he'd slapped his right one. "Fuckin' pussy."

Elwood and Richard thought this was hilarious.

Moosie shoved Harry. "Harry. Harry Balls."

Then Harry fucked up. He started to cry. And at that point, I was just glad it wasn't me. It was also at that moment that Moosie shifted his attention over my way.

The little shrimp glared at me. "What the fuck are you looking at?"

I couldn't help but stare back at him. I know, I'm an idiot, but I had such instant disrespect for his ignorance. This became my undoing.

The lines were drawn without me saying a word.

My first order of business in reporting to the new school was to visit the office and inform the secretary that I was new and in need of free hot lunch tickets. It was a government-sponsored deal for poor kids.

Right as I was handed the tickets, I looked over and saw Moosie walking by the plate glass. He locked onto me right away and stopped in his tracks—stared at me through the window.

He smiled.

Word spread pretty quickly who the poor kids were.

In the cafeteria at lunch, I sat alone at the end of a long flat table. I saw Moosie sit down with Richard and Elwood a couple of tables away. He mouthed "Watch this" to his goofs as he got up and sauntered over to my table.

He parked across from me and leaned in. "Hey. So I saw you at the bus stop this morning. What's your name?"

"Timothy." I hated my name. Timothy. Tim. Timid. It was such a pussy name. Thanks, mom.

"Tim," he mused. "Timmy. Hmm."

Hmm. I'd forgotten about Timmy. I countered with, "What's your name?"

"Moosie."

You gotta be kidding me. I couldn't help but smile. "Moosie. Nice name." Yeah, I'm a fuckin' idiot.

Moosie grinned and glanced over at Elwood and Richard. "I was just talking to my friends over there and we were wondering if you ever watched *The Man from U.N.C.L.E.*"

"Sometimes. When my mother isn't watching something else."

I'd said way too much. I don't know why I couldn't filter myself. Everything you gave them was ammunition and here I was offering up pearls before swine. In the logical recesses of my mind, I guess I always thought that if you were clever or could amuse a bully, they'd back off. But they don't appreciate your efforts because they're stupid to start with. They don't get the jokes.

Moosie knew he had an insecure fish on the line. He could smell it.

"What's your dad say about that?" he asked.

Always with the trick questions. I blurted out, "My dad's dead."

Idiot. I'd handed over the keys to the kingdom.

His interest picked up. "So you don't have a dad?"

Try for refreshingly honest? "No."

"And you don't have your own TV?"

So far, so bad. "No."

"And you get free lunch tickets," he summarized matter-of-fact.

I know I must have had a sick expression on my face because I felt sick to my stomach. I wished I'd starved instead of taking the free hot lunch. I wanted to scream at all these ingrates that it wasn't my fault my mother was a major fuckup.

Moosie smiled like the Grinch looking down on Whoville. "So…" He paused as dramatically as he could. "Are you poor?"

I didn't answer. I didn't have to.

Then he pulled a classic bully trick. And like Lucy with that stupid football she pulls away every time at the last minute, I Charlie Browned it.

Moosie's face softened like we could be friends. Like he wanted to share. Just out of the blue. That's always the first danger sign. I have no idea why I always fell for this. Maybe because I had a remote hope that I might not get my ass beat again. Sometimes, remote is better than nothing.

"So, on *U.N.C.L.E.*—who's your favorite—Napoleon or Illya?" he asked.

This seemed safe enough. "Illya."

He stood up and visually checked with his cohorts, then homed back in on me. "I knew you were gonna say that."

"You did?"

"Yeah. You know how I knew?"

I shook my head no.

"Cause Illya is a homo." He laughed and swaggered back to his buds who both smiled their approval.

The worst thing you could be was a homo.

I knew Illya wasn't a homo, but for some reason, I took it personal.

In homeroom, I stuck out like a sore thumb. The differences were obvious. For one, I was the only kid without a professional haircut. My shagginess stood out.

As if I needed to advertise my arrival, I'd tracked in large clods of mud under my shoes that led a straight path to my seat at the back of the room. I became the center of amusement when our battleaxe teacher Miss Barter slammed her book shut and strode down the aisle to my desk. She scowled down at me, then down at the clumps, then back at me. Back at the mud. Back at me. Her blood was boiling. It was everything she could do to control herself. Miss Barter was old school. We would not be having mess in her classroom.

She wagged a finger at me. "You need to get some moistened paper towels and clean this up immediately."

She turned on her heel, went back to her desk, flipped her book open and continued her lesson without missing a beat.

Kids either looked past you or sneered with malice when you had to do stuff like clean up mud on the floor. Especially when it was your own mud.

Scoping my surroundings at kneeling level put things in perspective for me. If there was any doubt about my financial status, I just had to compare shoes. Their shoes were shined, or brushed if they were Hush Puppies, and mine were worn out welfare issue with butter my mother smeared on them to make them look shiny.

Butter turns. After a while, your shoes smell funky. Bits of grass and dirt stuck to them.

I just had to make it through the next 2 weeks.

Yes, you're an asshole.

I came home from school to discover my mother ironing. She was not a big ironer so I knew something was up. Especially when I saw what she was pressing. A white uniform.

My mother was a licensed practical nurse, but she'd been out of it for a while. She was unnaturally up as she buffed out the wrinkles.

"What's going on?" I asked with great caution. Change involving my mother led to bad things more often than not.

"I got a job today," she beamed.

For a second, I was encouraged. Getting a job was a normal thing to do. But Mother wasn't known for normal.

"I start tomorrow," she continued as she adjusted the uniform surface on the ironing board. "Working in the hospital with elderly people. Terminal ones."

"Where is it?"

"A couple of miles down the road."

"How will you get there?"

"One of the nurses I'll be working the same schedule with drives right by on the main road. She said she'd pick me up and bring me home at night. She was really nice to me."

Something else was up. I just couldn't put my finger on it.

"And I've made a decision."

Oh, here we go.

"I'm going to go back to AA."

"That's good," my rote self said. Well, it was *kinda* good, except sometimes she made me go to the meetings. It wasn't all misery. The alkies could be funny, but mostly the meetings ended up sad and somber with resigned folks milling around an ancient coffee urn.

A part of me always fantasized that one day she would get her act together. Only problem was I'd seen this act before. Many times. She'd quit for a few days and try to eat real food. A few days is all it would last. It didn't take much to set her off and knock her off the wagon. And when she fell off, she didn't stick a toe in the water, she came back with a vengeance. It was never pretty. Everybody out of the pool.

"There's a meeting tomorrow night," she declared.

"Do I have to go?"

"No," she replied, concentrating on smoothing out a wrinkle.

That was good news. I shifted gears. "Can I watch TV?"

"Yeah, go ahead, there's nothing on."

I found an Elvis movie. I liked Elvis movies because they were dependable. There'd be hip-swingin'. Some curling of the upper lip. And of course, the obligatory I-didn't-start-it-but-I'm-going-to-finish-it fight scene. In between singing a song every six minutes, Elvis always had time to work in a fight.

The peanut gallery started up behind me. "You know he doesn't even play his own guitar."

God. Couldn't she ever shut up? I didn't bite. That didn't stop her.

"They tried to teach him, but he's too stupid to learn it."

He looks like he's doing better than you I thought to myself, wishing I dared to say it out loud.

The fight scene started. Elvis took one on the chin. Then another. It looked grim. But Elvis bounced back and knocked his opponent senseless.

"That's all fake. You can tell."

It was endless. I gave up and went to my room, shutting the door behind me.

I dozed off reading a *Famous Monsters* article about Karloff. Forrest J Ackerman asked Boris if he liked children. Boris replied that he loved children.

Boiled.

That was a chuckler.

I heard loud snoring from the living room. That was my signal it was safe to get something to eat. I went out to the kitchen, passing my passed out parental guidance sawing a cord of wood, slumped over in her chair wearing a bathrobe that gaped at the top exposing one of her flabby breasts.

She'd made cookies.

My mother had a penchant for making cookies. The only problem was she was drunk all the time and she'd forget how long the cookies had been in the oven. Her batches were always burned. Always. She blamed it on the stove being erratic, but that was pretty easy to see through.

These were extra burned on the bottom. Charcoal. Nasty.

I fished around in the silverware drawer and found a butter knife. I had to scrape pretty hard to get the hard black stuff off. But it was worth it.

They were peanut butter and the tops were still good.

I reclined on my bed with a cheap black and silver handheld transistor radio mashed against my left ear. I tried to use the tiny off-white hard plastic ear piece, but after just 5 minutes jammed in my ear, it hurt. So I played it right into my ear.

I'd discovered that even up in Maine, at night, I could pull in a barely intelligible WABC all the way from New York City. They played Beatles. And not just the hits. Sure, they'd rightfully play the hell out of *Hey Jude*, but they weren't afraid to stick a little *Dear Prudence* or *Glass Onion* on their playlist.

They'd played *While My Guitar Gently Weeps* the previous hour. They were spinning *Ob-La-Di, Ob-La-Da* when my mother knocked on the door.

"Turn that down in there!"

She had some kind of weird radar. How could she hear it? *I* barely could.

"It *is* turned down," I kind of yelled back.

I heard her slump against the door. "I can still hear it."

God! I turned it down.

"Go to bed," I advised.

I thought I heard her move away from the door to grapple her way down the hallway, but I was wrong.

Seconds of silence ticked by.

I turned the radio back up in my ear.

She jiggled the door handle. "I can still hear it in there."

I put my pillow over my head to muffle the sound.

She swung the door open with, "I hear it."

I lost my composure and angrily switched the transistor off, and when I did, the white annotated on-off dial broke off inside the radio. I pulled the pillow away from my head and bounced the radio off the end of the bed where it ricocheted onto the floor.

"There. Happy now?"

My mother didn't say anything. I waited for her rebuke. Nothing. Too pissed out of her gourd. Not enough energy to fight. She thudded her left shoulder into the door frame as she tried to clear her way out of my room.

She left my door open and shuffled away into the dark.

She stood over me.

I'd fallen asleep reading *Famous Monsters* ads and hadn't heard her come in. When I realized she was in the room, I made sure to keep my eyes closed.

She reeked. I wondered if the future AA meeting she'd announced earlier in the evening was still in the cards or if she'd already made up her mind to flip. I pretended to be asleep. She weaved over me breathing heavily for what seemed like minutes.

"Timmy," she whispered.

I refused to acknowledge.

"Timmy," she said out loud.

I continued to play dead.

"I might be sick. And I need you if I'm gonna be sick."

She hung over me waiting for a response.

I refused to give her one.

As she skulked away, I wished she'd go back to bed and choke on her own vomit.

Fuck you.

Asshole.

Harry Balls

I tried to time my arrival at the bus stop the next morning so I got there at the very last second. I needed to minimize my face-time with Moosie and his hooligans.

For some reason, they were hands off on the bus. Maybe they were formulating their plan for lunch.

I stood in the cafeteria line being patient. As I approached the serving window, Moosie, Elwood and Richard skirted up alongside and jostled their way in front of me.

Okay. Keep your mouth shut. Let this go.

"Hey," I heard myself say.

Moosie shot back with, "Shut up, welfare boy."

I knew better than to spar.

I carried my tray as far away as I could and sat off by myself. Still they sought me out. Moosie ambled over with Elwood in tow.

Moosie elbowed Elwood and said, "Hey, Timmy. I hope you're enjoyin' that free lunch."

He reached over and took my open milk carton from my tray. "So what are we havin' today? Some milk? You like milk?"

He spit into my milk.

"I asked you a question, Timmy. You like milk?"

Without making eye contact, I replied, "Yeah."

Moosie poured the milk all over the food on my tray and bounced the empty carton off my forehead. "Well, have some milk then."

He turned to Elwood and then back to me. "Oh, and I'd like you to meet Elwood."

Moosie nodded to Elwood who reached over and flipped my tray upside down into my lap.

Moosie feigned a look of disgust. "Maybe you should pay for your lunch like everybody else, you moocher."

Elwood threw his two cents in. "Better clean that mess up before you get in trouble."

As they walked off sowing arrogance, I wished there was someone I could tell.

But if someone tried to help, that made it worse in the long run.

Then you were really in for it.

It was the next to last day of school before summer vacation.

After the final bell, kids waited in the parking lot for the bus to arrive. The transportation wasn't consistent. You might wait 5 minutes or you might wait twenty. But if you weren't there when they pulled up, they left without you.

I walked down the hill from the school to the parking lot.

Elwood and Richard had poor little Harry anchored while Moosie sat on top of him, pounding away mercilessly. Like I said, I felt sorry for Harry, but I was glad it was him and not me.

The bus finally arrived.

Moosie dismounted and gave the signal to his buddies they could let Harry up. Harry struggled to his feet and staggered to the bus door, waiting desperately for it to open. Bus drivers never seemed to notice jack shit. Eventually the ace behind the wheel opened the door while staring straight ahead.

Harry was about to hop up into the bus when Moosie hauled off and kicked his ass so hard, it crumpled Harry into a fetal position between the top two steps.

"What you waitin' for, Harry Balls?" Moosie chided.

The odor spread quickly on the ride home.

Harry was on the verge of throwing up and shitting simultaneously. He marshaled all of his super powers to keep himself in check, because if they broke you, it was over.

Kids scrunched up their faces and plugged their noses.

"Oh, damn!" Moosie exclaimed in mock horror. "Is that *you*, Harry Balls?"

Elwood couldn't resist his personal stranglehold on the obvious. "What'd you do—shit your pants?"

It took an eternity for the bus to get to our stop. Harry rose from his seat and waddled down the aisle, holding his ass cheeks together with all his might.

Richard plugged his nose. "Somethin' stinks! What is that?"

Harry stayed focused on his exit strategy.

Moosie stuck out a foot and tripped him, then manifested fake concern. "Harry Balls! Go home and wash your ass! Man!"

I had to give it to Harry. He could take a punch. He righted himself and tried to complete the gauntlet.

Next came the unspeakable. As Harry made it to the front of the bus, turds fell out of his left pant leg into the aisle before he could make it down the steps to freedom.

Some kids screamed in laughter and others gagged. Moosie pointed and howled along with Elwood and Richard. "He shit his pants!"

Harry's face turned crimson as he made his way off.

In a weird kind of way, at that moment in time, I hated Harry, too.

I just didn't know why.

The Last Day of School

Harry didn't show up the next morning for the last day of school. Couldn't say as I blamed him, but I would have relished the distraction of him being Moosie's punching bag.

Moosie and his mates stood off to the side smoking Winstons. They laughed conspiratorially.

I tried to blend into the scenery without looking queer.

Moosie meandered over and blew smoke in my face. "Hey, Timmy."

"Hey."

Moosie grabbed my wrist and I wrenched it back. "Leave me alone."

He grabbed my wrist again. I tried to pull away, but Richard came up from behind and doubled me over with a half-nelson. Moosie forced my free hand to hit my own face. I bucked and Richard clamped down even more. I was in severe discomfort. I was convinced this gorilla was going to snap my arm or something. Moosie continued to slap me with my own hand.

"Hey, tiny Tim. Relax," Moosie said. "You're gonna hurt yourself."

Richard and Elwood were in hysterics. Moosie gave me a final solid slap with my own hand. Thank God the bus rolled up. Moosie let my wrist go and Richard and Elwood retreated.

Moosie taunted me. "See you at school, Timmy."

Gym class. I fucking hated it.

It wasn't that I didn't want or couldn't use the physical outlet, I just didn't want to be in competition about it. And being the littlest kid except for Moosie didn't play out in my favor.

The gym teachers I had were sometimes nice, but mostly they were jutting jaw militaristic clowns who failed at making the grade as a professional athlete. We knew how the saying went. "Those who can't *do*, teach, and those who can't *teach*, teach gym."

Gym teachers made no bones about how they felt about you and those vibes were echoed by their jock favorites. As soon as I suited up and reported to the gymnasium, it was all these muscular hunks could do to even be in the same room with me.

Picking teams was the worst. The gym teacher started by selecting the two biggest letter guys as the team captains and they got to alternate choosing who they wanted to be on their team. I was *always* picked last. Hands down. And even when I was the only choice left, the ass who had to take me chafed.

They rolled their eyes like it was the end of the world and grimaced, "Okay, I'll take Tim."

Hey, fuck you, assholes. I can't change how I was fucking *born*, okay?

Showers were mandatory. It made you vulnerable because the coach wasn't anywhere to be found in the locker room.

I put on my gym clothes as quickly as possible. They had official school-color gym uniforms, but if you couldn't afford one, you were allowed to wear a T-shirt and dark shorts instead. I was the only one without a proper uniform.

Just as I finished lacing my sneakers, Richard plopped himself down on the bench next to me. "Hey. Peckerhead. You and me. Parking lot after school."

My mouth hung open. "For what?"

"Just be there, carrot-top." With that, he stood and walked away.

I was never sure what I'd done to provoke these jackasses, but there was definitely something about me they didn't like.

After school, I stealthed my way to the waiting area for the bus. Moosie and his sidekicks were screwing around on the lawn. I'd watched cowardly from behind some bushes until I saw the bus coming up the street. I thought timing my entrance just right would spare me some wrath. As I got closer, Richard fingered me.

Moosie and his cohorts formed a circle around me as the bus pulled up. I moved toward the bus. Moosie blocked me and turned to his crew.

"Hold him."

Richard and Elwood each grabbed an arm. I struggled initially, but it was always pointless, so I gave up without much of a fight, but I managed to fire off a "Leave me alone!"

Moosie smiled. "Sure."

He hauled off and belted me hard in the stomach.

The punch knocked the wind out of me. Still, I couldn't help but let my mouth get the best of me. "You're a piece of shit."

Moosie raised an eyebrow. "Really?"

He kicked me square in the balls.

I spit up a bit.

"Next year, fucker," he warned. "I'll be waiting, poor boy."

Moosie nodded to his underlings to let me go and they did. Trained monkeys.

I fell to my knees, nauseous as hell. Afraid I was going to lose my cookies. Summoning Richard and Elwood, Moosie cackled as he mounted the steps of the bus.

Nobody ever intervened to save you. Just ask Harry.

I picked myself up off the ground.

That night in our trailer, my mother popped another in a series of Pabst Blue Ribbons as I sullenly looked on. She loved to lecture me. Always brimming over with useless advice.

"Keep your distance," she'd say. "Stay away from him."

Parents acted like you were seeking bullies out.

No.

They found *you*.

Dorothy

It was hot out. Humid heat accompanied by a hazy cricket buzz so loud it fused into an over-sized insect sound effect from a '50s science fiction movie. One week into my summer vacation, I sat bored out of my mind on the steps leading up to the side door of our tin can. I stayed close to home intentionally to minimize the risk of meeting Moosie and his clowns in the neighborhood.

My mother worked during the day so I was left to my own devices a lot. A latchkey kid. For the most part, parents I knew thought nothing of leaving relatively young kids home alone because we were terrified of fucking up. We lived in an age of corporal punishment to include a strap administered by your school principal. And the strap was just the appetizer. Your parents beat you more severely after you got home.

I'd prayed summer would last forever and during the month of June, it seemed to do just that. There was no one to hang out with. I was climbing the walls. Plus there was a monster horsefly annoying the fuck out of me.

I heard a soft female voice. "Hey."

I looked up. Didn't see anybody.

"Hey!" accompanied by a sexy half-laugh.

She was calling from behind a screened window in the more luxurious brown and white trailer next door. I had trouble making her out. She leaned closer to the screen and her face came into view—a gorgeous brunette girl-next-door. Great smile.

"Do you baby-sit?"

I stood up, wiped the dust off my ass, and stepped over some weeds to stand closer to her window. I squinted and tried to get a better look. "I don't know. I guess so."

She disappeared with, "Come around to the other side."

I made my way around as instructed and found myself at the base of the stairs leading up to her tiny porch.

Dorothy stepped out onto the deck sporting a summer print dress that showed off her all-feminine shape. 21 years old. Wow. She was the total package.

"I need a favor. I'll pay you."

Anything. Just name it. I was instantly in love.

She motioned me up the stairs and pulled me inside where her 1-year-old stood grinning and bouncing, hanging off the railing of his playpen situated in the center of the living room.

"Listen, I have an appointment and my sitter canceled. Can you watch Gene? Please? For just a couple of hours. That's all, I swear."

"Yeah, I guess so."

"Oh, my God, thank you," she gushed. "You're a life-saver." And she was out the door. I followed and watched from the porch.

"Hey, what's your name?"

She laughed and lightly slapped her forehead. "Oh, yeah. Sorry. It's Dorothy," she said as she slid into her car. She cranked up the engine, flashed her pearly-whites at me, and tore out of her short gravel driveway.

Dorothy. What a beautiful name. I didn't even know her and I was in love with all of the possibilities. I was on cloud nine. She'd thanked me. She thought I was a life-saver.

I turned back to Gene. He was cute.

He smiled and gurgled and so did I.

Little Gene wasn't any trouble. He cooed the whole time and seemed to be unconditionally happy. "Hey, kid, anytime you want to trade mothers, let me know," I cracked.

I went through Dorothy's records. I handled each one like it was the Mona Lisa. If you had 20 or 30 albums in your collection, that was a fair amount. Dorothy had at least a hundred. She was big on Motown soul and was apparently a Neil Diamond fan—whoever the hell he was. She had lots of Beatles. Including the 45 single *The Ballad of John and Yoko.* I knew about it, but had never actually heard the song because it was banned from the radio.

I slipped the vinyl out of its paper picture sleeve and lifted the lid on Dorothy's console stereo. It was a better than average record player. Personally, I'd be pissed if someone messed with my equipment, but I was unable to control myself. I had to hear this song. I snapped the 45 adapter ring into the center of the record and placed it on the turntable. I figured out the controls and put the stylus on the groove.

I kept the volume low so I could hear Dorothy if she drove up. I listened studiously with one ear up against the speakers. This song was badass. Between replays, I checked to see if Dorothy was coming.

When I was done, I put the record back just the way I'd found it.

In all honesty, I wanted to take it, but I already liked Dorothy too much and I didn't even know her.

When she returned, she handed me a five-dollar bill.

"Oh, thanks," I said as I pocketed the money.

"Is that enough?" she asked.

The going rate for a girl I'd lived near the year before was 50 cents an hour—a dollar an hour if the parents were feeling generous. And that was for multiple kids. I hadn't even been there an hour and a half. "Oh, yeah. No, that's great."

Things were working out. Now I had enough to buy my own copy of *The Ballad of John and Yoko*.

She flashed her million-dollar smile. "Can I call you again?"

"What?" *What?* Did I just say that? God, I sounded like an idiot.

"If I need you again, would you mind?"

"Oh, no. Not at all."

My mother decided to make it a Madame Butterfly night.

From an early age, I learned to hate any opera my mother chose to butcher, but Puccini's tragedy was her favorite. My mother fancied herself a singer and a good—no, *great* singer at that. Maybe she could approximate the vocals in her fractured youth, but as early as her 30s, her pipes had been destroyed by the ravages of liquor. The fact that she burped through the high notes never seemed to deter her. The drunker she got, the more she got into it. "I'll get that note next time," she'd slur with ice clinking loudly in her highball glass.

It was quite a show. Not one you wanted to see, but certainly one she wasn't bashful about inviting you to. I wanted to crawl under my bed and hide every time she dragged out the multi-record set in its tattered taped-up box which contained several brittle and heavily scratched 78 RPM records and a well-worn libretto she no longer needed because she was an expert at fucking up Puccini's masterpiece from memory.

When our mono RCA Victor record player croaked, my mother was ecstatic to find a chintzy stereo at Ward's that had a stylus on one side to play 45s and LPs, and when you flipped the stylus over, it had a noticeably larger needle to play 78 RPMs. She was delighted she could still play her old records. I was mortified. They didn't even *make* 78s anymore, but my mother had lucked out.

I knew I was in trouble when I came home and the record player was already set up. This meant two things. One, I was about to be assaulted again by a toasted Madame Butterfly, and two, I'd be there a while. Madame Butterfly was an opera that seemed to go on for days. This also meant I wouldn't be "borrowing" the stereo anytime soon to listen to my handful of records in my closet with the door closed.

I wished she'd just pass out in front of *Hawaii 5-O* or Carol Burnett. I could always hope she'd find something "good" on TV and give up on the concert idea before it came to fruition. But usually if she'd dragged out the equipment, you were in for the complete show.

It was not my night. She was going to summon the ghost of Cio-Cio San once again. Out came the special rainbow-colored dress with golden accents. She studied herself in a bathroom mirror as she carefully arranged her bun and secured her hair in place with a pair of chopsticks she'd pocketed at a Chinese restaurant. She even applied the clown-white face make-up.

And of course, who could forget the knife? It was the biggest blade we had, a dull 9-inch butcher knife. My mother never used it to chop anything up in the kitchen, so maybe it was purchased exclusively for her performances.

The TV went off unceremoniously, her excitement palpable. I had to take my seat in front of her as the audience. And goddammit, I'd *better* like the show. There was always a tense silence punctuated by my mother scratching her way through numerous attempts to plant the stylus onto the outer edge of the record without gouging it.

Christ, this was endless. At least she wasn't inviting neighborhood kids in like she'd done at previous locations we'd escaped from. Thank God I hadn't made any friends yet.

Ten minutes in, she stumbled against the record player as she poured another two fingers during an orchestral fill. The needle tore across the entire platter, bounced up onto the paper label, ricocheted off the spindle, and dive-bombed into the center of the platter, pitting and scratching it more than it was already. The tone arm skipped 3 times and settled into the groove.

This set the old lady off. "Goddam-Jesus-Mary-Mother-of-God-Son-of-a-bitch-Bastard!" Even when she was mad, she never said "fuck." I thought that was a pretty interesting delineation given her propensity to turn profanity-laced stream of consciousness outbursts into high art.

For some reason, I lost my cool. I stood up for effect. Even at 13, I was taller than her five foot frame. I declared I wasn't interested in listening to her arias anymore. I'd had it. And for some reason, I felt a need to stoke the fire, which was really stupid on my part. I told her I'd made some babysitting money and I was going to go out and buy the *Ballad of John and Yoko* single so I could listen to some *real* music.

You never attacked her opera. That just wasn't done. It was enough that parents barely tolerated your tastes. You were supposed to be happy with that compromise. But I'd had enough. If I had to listen to her shit, I sure as hell wasn't going to be stopped from listening to what gave me pleasure.

A loud exchange corkscrewed as my mother chased me down the short hallway into my bedroom. "I will not have you spending money on those two awful people!"

"Why not?" I yelled back.

"They say the word 'Christ' for Chrissakes!"

"So what? You say it all the time!"

"Goddammit! I have had it with your goddam back talk—you're getting too many ideas from these goddam rock and roll musicians! You will not bring that sonofabitchin' record into this house!"

I slammed my bedroom door in her face, making sure to twist the doorknob lock. I hurled myself down on the bed and buried my head in the pillow.

She came at the door in a heartbeat, trying to jimmy it open. When she realized it was locked, she slapped the smooth veneer with her open hand. "I'm thinking of sending you to church!" she hollered.

That was a valid threat. She'd sentenced me before to church services on Sundays and I hated it. It's not like she ever went with me. She used whatever local church would send some total stranger to come pick me up. It was a built-in babysitter for a couple of hours. I was fortunate that none of the casual acquaintances she involved me with ever turned out to be predators. In retrospect, that was just the luck of the draw.

Eventually she gave up and went back to the living room. No more pounding on the door. I punched my pillow again, with open hostility.

I don't even know why I asked her permission.

I didn't go buy the record. I was mad at myself for not busting out. She wouldn't have known either way, but for some reason, I listened to and obeyed my mother for the most part.

That's just what you did.

But it was getting tougher.

Steve Oreno

Timing is everything. A miracle fell from the sky. Someone had taken up residence in the old *Pupp's Good Eats*. He had a brand new hand-painted sign: *Steve Oreno's Pizza Joint*.

I walked across the loose gravel parking lot and went in the first hour he opened his doors. There was a counter and a few tables and not much else except the used Seeburg 45 jukebox over in one of the corners. The joint was bare bones, but the floors were swept and the tables were clean.

I was the only one there for the grand opening. I sat down at the counter.

Steve Oreno stepped out from the kitchen in back. He was in his early 30s with strong, sculpted muscles underneath a tight t-shirt. Jeans. Workman boots. His jet-black hair was waved back into a perfect ducktail. Steve was full of life, a character, Italian through and through, with the hand gestures and everything. He reminded me of a young Tony Curtis—a bull with a killer twinkle in his eyes.

"Hey, my friend, what can I get you?"

I liked him immediately. "Small pepperoni pizza and a Coke."

"Coming right up."

He hustled into the back and I watched him from my perch at the counter. He kept his back to me as he pulled out ingredients from an industrial refrigerator and set them on his prep table. He talked over his shoulder while he worked. Told me he only used fresh ingredients. He took out a slab of dough and tossed it. I'd never seen that done except on TV. This kind of live entertainment was unheard of in the Styx of Maine. He was really proud of his tossing talent—told me it made a crust that was lighter. Crisp. And when it was hand-spun, the irregularity made for each bite being a slightly different eating experience. Yeah, he was into it.

Without missing a beat, he reached into an old-fashioned fire-engine red Coke cooler stocked with 16-ounce thick green-glass bottles shoved up to their necks in shaved ice. Using an opener, he snapped the top off effortlessly and set the bottle down in front of me in one motion.

He went back to work in the kitchen, chopping up onions and green peppers. At one point, he leaned over to reach for a container and his t-shirt rode up exposing the small of his back above the waistline of his Lee's. There were large gouges of flesh gone from right above his hips. The skin was all one color—healed, but misshapen. Very noticeable. It sure didn't look like any wounds I'd ever seen.

He caught me looking at his backside and pulled his t-shirt down.

"So what happened to you?" I asked innocently.

Gotta love youth. No filters.

He hesitated. "On my back?"

"Yeah."

He dismissed me by making himself busy wiping pepperoni and shredded mozzarella remnants off the counter into a hand that relayed them to a nearby trash can.

I continued to stare.

He looked back at me with no twinkle. There was a darkness in his eyes, but not mean black holes like Moosie had. Steve looked like he'd seen things he'd wished he'd never seen. Matter of factly, he said, "I got hit by a rocket that exploded near me."

I was aware there was a war going on in Vietnam. And on some level, I knew Steve was a survivor with stories to tell, but the rest of me didn't connect the dots. I got up from my stool and walked over to scope out the jukebox.

Steve watched me and called from the kitchen. "Yeah, check it out."

He had quite a selection—everything from The Archies' *Sugar, Sugar* to Glen Campbell's *Wichita Lineman.* Not saying you wouldn't listen to those, but you were borderline homo if someone caught you liking those particular selections. There was a lot of stuff I'd never heard of. Creedence Clearwater Revival. Blood, Sweat & Tears. I mean, what the hell was a Three Dog Night? And there was this Neil Diamond guy again.

But Steve had the good stuff, too. Beatles. 45s that you loved on both sides. *Hey Jude* backed with *Revolution. Get Back* and *Don't Let Me Down.* I kept reading down the little flimsy cardboard title cards. Searching. Hoping. And there it was. I'll be damned. *The Ballad of John and Yoko* and George Harrison's *Old Brown Shoe*. Son. Of. A. Bitch.

Steve saw me fish a dime out of my pocket and tried to help me out. "Two bits gets you 3 plays."

I laughed to myself. Steve. Two bits. Nobody said that anymore. I swapped my dime out for a quarter and slipped it into the machine. The Seeburg lit up like it wanted to come out for a spin.

"I hope you don't mind, but I'm going to play the same song three times."

"Depends on what it is."

"*Ballad of John and Yoko.*"

Steve didn't comment until I queued up another three plays of my favorite Beatles' song of the moment.

"Jesus Christ. Can't you mix it up a little? I've heard it so many times now, I want to jump off a bridge. Play some Marvin Gaye. Smokey Robinson. Some Stevie Wonder. Sly and the Family Stone."

"I don't know who any of those people are."

Steve's jaw dropped. "What?" He said it like I might be stupid.

A timer dinged and Steve vanished into the kitchen. I leaned sideways off my stool so I could see what he was doing. Using an extra-wide spatula, he guided my pizza out of a hot oven and edged it straight onto a waiting pan. He produced a pizza cutter out of thin air and with three distinct and powerful slices coupled with laser-beam accuracy, cut that pie into 6 perfectly proportioned pieces. Bam, bam, bam. Done. He spirited the tray off the prep table and in one move, about-faced, stepped up to the counter and slid my piping hot food down to nestle next to my Coke.

I told Steve I made money babysitting. He thought I was an idiot for putting all my spare money into the Seeburg so I could hear *The Ballad of John and Yoko* continuously.

"What's wrong with you?" he asked with his devilish smile.

"What do you mean?"

"For all the quarters you've plugged into that jukebox, you could have bought your own copy of that stupid record."

"My mom says I can't have it."

Steve looked at me incredulously. "Fuck her. Go buy it."

Those simple words he uttered spoke volumes to me. We'd barely met and he'd used a four-letter word in my presence. An adult talking to me like a peer was a new experience. Profanity was rampant in my mother's domain, but vulgarity was something altogether different. It got your attention. Here was a seemingly normal likeable adult who was encouraging me to rebel. He couldn't have picked a better day to turn on that light switch in my head.

Steve softened. "Okay, you play your *Ballad of John and Yoko*. Enjoy it. As you should."

Steve wiped a crumb off the counter, flapped the dish towel over his shoulder, and popped the drawer on his ancient cash register to reach in for a quarter. He flipped the two bits in the air and caught the coin like he was going to do something really special with it.

"But first...you ain't leavin' until we work on expanding your musical horizons."

I wasn't sure how this was gonna go, but I trusted in his wisdom and I can't tell you why I did that. I just knew he would never do anything to hurt me. Because above all, he seemed fair.

That made me game for whatever he was talking about.

The Wonder Bike

I was babysitting little Gene, pawing through Dorothy's records. I pulled out the *Ballad of John and Yoko* single. I loved everything The Beatles ever did, but I was particularly infatuated with this piece of forbidden fruit because to me it was the epitome of rock and roll. It was dangerous.

I slipped the record under my shirt, finding myself with the devil on one shoulder and an angel on the other. I pulled the record out from under my shirt and put it back. A momentary lapse. I couldn't steal from Dorothy. Why was I even thinking that way?

I was broke. All my babysitting money went through my fingers up at Steve Oreno's. And right when I needed to find a way to get more money in my pocket, I met a temporary friend. The kind you only need for roughly 5 minutes.

Opportunity knocked. Bouncing Gene on one hip, I opened the door. A brainy looking kid about my age stood on Dorothy's steps.

He peered over his thick black-framed glasses, surprised to see me. "Oh, I'm sorry. I was looking for…"

"She's not here," I explained.

"Oh. Well, no problem." He stuck out a welcoming hand and we shook. "I'm Fred, by the way."

He didn't look like a Fred. He was clean-cut. Well dressed. Even his jeans were ironed.

"I deliver the paper here and I was in the neighborhood, so I thought I'd stop by to collect the subscription money. No sweat. I can come by some other time."

He bopped down the steps, stopped and turned back to me. "Hey. You want a job?" he asked out of the blue.

What?

He didn't let my "What?" look stop him. "My family's moving in a couple of weeks and they still need someone to pick up my route. You interested?"

Yeah, I was. "Sounds good, but I don't have any way to get around."

"Oh, I can help you with that," he smiled. Fred was unnaturally cheerful, but otherwise he seemed harmless. "I can *sell* you a bike."

I knew that expense was out of the question. He saw it in my eyes.

"Trust me. I have just the bike for you."

The next morning, after delivering his papers, Fred came around with my new means of transportation. He'd built it himself—a heavy-framed bare-bones pedal-driven fender-less masterpiece he dubbed "The Wonder Bike." I got the whole package for $5 and he deferred that until I got my first week's wages. It was a rickety contraption, but it would hold together. Fred guaranteed it.

Thus began my tenure as a paperboy.

I got up at o'dark-thirty. Early early. The newspaper distributor dumped the stack of bound papers on a street corner. They were always there waiting for you. I used a small crummy serrated knife out of our kitchen drawer to cut open the bundle. I'd sling my heavy canvas bag over my shoulder, stuff it carefully with the daily news, and head off into my neighborhoods. I had 40 people on my route.

The daily editions were heavy enough that the canvas strap on my bag sawed a friction burn into whatever shoulder was bearing the weight. But the worst was the Sunday edition. Thank God not everyone wanted those 2-inch thick copies—it was like hauling bricks around. I couldn't carry the Sundays all at once, so after cutting my bundle on the street corner, I'd hoist what I could lift without making myself so lop-sided the bike wobbled out of balance. I'd come back an hour later and the untouched part of the newspaper stack was there waiting unmolested. No one ever ripped them off.

I liked being a paperboy, but I hated collecting the subscription money. The main office forced me to be a combination delivery boy/bill collection agency. The news people didn't bill the customer, they made the little scrawny paperboy be the foil, begging customers for money they owed. If you didn't get the money, you didn't get your ten-percent commission. The subscription was a dollar a week, not counting the Sunday edition. A lot of people passed on including the Sunday rag because the extra 35 cents was cost prohibitive.

At the end of every week, my commission and measly tips put a whole six or seven bucks in my pocket. Don't get me wrong. I was happy to have it. It was freedom at a low level, but freedom nonetheless.

It was dark outside when I started deliveries, and needless to say, for only $5, the Wonder Bike did not come with a headlight. On rainy days, with no fenders for protection, mud sprayed up around the tires and painted two distinct lines up my middle in the back and two more in the front.

I was a good paperboy. I never threw the paper into the bushes or on the sidewalk. Nope. I folded them up nicely and walked right up to your house and placed them either inside the outer storm door or in your mailbox. I went the extra mile.

And still people would screw me over for the money— shutting off their lights when they saw me coming up the walk. Some wouldn't pay me for a month at a time. And these weren't poor people. They were professional curmudgeons.

There was one old crab who waited every morning for me to open her screen door. I'd carefully place her paper and the moment I left her porch, she'd fling her inner door open and go off. "It's 5:35! I expect my paper before 5:30!"

Part of me was shamed into feeling like I was letting her down and not doing my job and another part of me just wanted her to shut the fuck up and pay her bill on time instead of making me wait. Like I said, the meanest jackasses were also the most stingy.

I enjoyed some parts of the job.

There was the mom and pop donut shop. I could smell those intoxicating vapors as I skipped up their walkway. About once a week, they handed me a fresh warm delight as I dropped off the morning news at their main counter. The plain donuts were out of this world, but the cinnamon-sugared ones were my favorite. Plus they tipped you a friggin' quarter along with the treat. Good eats plus three more *Ballad of John and Yoko* plays.

Although the Sunday papers were a bitch to transport, there were a handful of people at an old folks' home that I didn't mind visiting. The Sunday news was the only delivery they got all week and that thick paper was cash on the barrel head. Instant coin in the pocket. And if that wasn't enough, they were good tippers to boot. These folks had nothing going for them except tubes running up their noses and they'd press 2 quarters into your hand with a smile.

The elderly all wanted someone to talk to because they were so lonely. Dying. Every so often, I'd show up and a customer's bed would be empty. Gone. Nobody ever told me they died, I just knew. But I never got stiffed with an unsold paper—there was always someone who would take it and become your new dying customer.

Sometimes they wanted to sit with me. I kind of hated it when they asked me to stay, but I did anyway. They'd reach out and gently stroke the side of my face with the backs of their withered, age-spotted hands.

I also delivered to the front desk of the hospital my mother nursed in. The receptionist was always nice to me. I think the word was out that my mother was crazy.

Delivering to the old folks home and the hospital was a lot of effort for the return.

Let's just say it wasn't as glamorous as it sounds.

I spent more and more Sunday afternoons at Steve O's. He took those opportunities to school me.

The food and drink was on me, but the education was on him. His money, his music. My good fortune.

He didn't mind playing Elvis and The Beatles. But he knew how to mix it up. Soul. Rock. Pop. Country. He threw out names of artists in Dorothy's collection. The Temptations. Sam and Dave. Smokey Robinson.

He enjoyed schooling me and I was a willing pupil.

Mother

My mother was not a good cook, but I imagine she would have been better at it if she could have set the bottle down on occasion. She was never prepared to do any in-depth chef work. Our cupboards were normally bare and the refrigerator often hosted nothing more than an opened bottle of Moxie soda. I guess she felt safe buying Moxie because she knew I wouldn't drink what amounted to a bitter sugarless Coke.

I ate meals that consisted of nothing more than a bowl of rice with milk on it. One afternoon I came home to an ungodly smell wafting as far as three trailers away. She was cooking turnip soup. I use the term cooking loosely. The old lady had thrown a whole turnip into a pot of boiling water. She proudly served me the broth and I promptly turned up my nose. Oddly enough, even though we didn't always have money for food, dollars fell out of the sky for beer and liquor purchases.

If she was really in her cups, food could become her weapon of choice. Literally. When I was in the 4th grade, she burned me when she burst into the bathroom while I was taking a bath. She waved a bowl of corn chowder around as she chastised me for using too much shampoo. Without warning, with a big sweep of her arm, she threw it all over me and screamed, "Clean it up! Clean it up!"

It took me over an hour to remove bits of corn chowder off of myself, the walls, the floor, and the bathtub. I was too angry to cry. I hated her too much for that.

A trick she loved to pull out of the hat was to send me to bed with no supper. She used that one a lot. To me, it was never about punishment. She wanted me out of the festivities. She wanted evenings where she didn't have to address her mistakes. She wanted time to herself. Plus it alleviated her responsibility as a provider. No mess, no fuss.

Sorry I got in the way.

She could punish me all she wanted. What was the worst that happened? My stomach growled and I curled up on my bed in an effort to stave off boredom in the darkness.

I wasn't about to break.

My mother jiggled my bedroom doorknob. I looked at my wind-up alarm clock. 8:17 PM. What the fuck. I undid the lock and opened the door.

She had a crazed look in her eyes. Okay, her *normal* look, but jacked up a bit.

"Get your shoes on," she instructed.

We trudged along in silence. Our mission: Acquire a six-pack of cheap 16-ouncers and a meatball sandwich, which would later be solely consumed by my mother without a thought to me being minus dinner. She never shared. I was just expected to be an accomplice and endure.

We walked because we didn't have a car. She managed to sponge off her co-worker when it came to rides to and from work, but when it came to beer runs, we were on our own.

She was already tanked, making sure to quaff her last brew just prior to us setting out on our quest.

On our way to the nearest convenience store, we passed a small private funeral home. She got a wild hair, her eyes darting. "Let's go inside."

She led me in. There was some stiff laid out in an open casket for viewing. We didn't know him. No one was there. Just us and this dead guy.

She took my elbow and edged me up to the side of the coffin.

She looked through me with her crazy eyes. "I don't want you to be afraid of dead people."

In my mind, that had never been an issue with me because I'd never been around a dead body. Until now. This was new territory.

"Touch him," she said.

Excuse me?

She saw me hesitate and touched him herself, poking his side. "Go ahead. Touch him. It's not that bad."

I held back. Even at 13, I knew this was insane shit.

She took hold of my wrist and pawed my hand on his chest. What the fuck.

"See?" she marveled. "It's not that bad."

At the convenience store, she took pity and bought me a Zero bar. That was my supper.

Her meatball sandwich smelled delicious the moment she unwrapped it in our kitchen. She thought nothing of eating both halves in front of me without offering as much as a bite.

Yes, I hate you.

And then I met Elvis...

I was starting to enjoy a relatively lucrative summer. I had my paper route money and Dorothy was throwing me a fair amount of babysitting gigs, which were always a breeze because Gene was irrepressibly happy.

It was a Tuesday afternoon shortly after lunch and I was playing Dorothy's *White Album*. She'd given me formal permission to play her stereo while she was out since she didn't own a TV, which was odd—I didn't know anyone who didn't have one. But Dorothy was different in so many ways. High on life.

She'd watched me handle the delicate process of removing and returning records to their protective sleeves— observed me when I placed the vinyl platters on the turntable. Hers had automatic cueing, so you just had to twist a knob to make the tone arm move over the beginning of the record and gently lower the stylus down. I had respect for this privilege because it allowed me freedom I wasn't used to having. Dorothy expected and trusted me to be careful and I was.

I'd just put on side 3, rocking out to *Birthday*. Gene loved the beat. He grabbed hold of the edge of his playpen and squealed harmony out at the top of his lungs. I jacked up the sound and he squealed louder.

I heard a tractor-trailer rumble to a stop outside. I peeked out the kitchen window. Someone was moving in. Their trailer had seen some moves, but it was big and sturdy.

A car pulled up alongside. A father and son got out. They didn't match in body type, but I could tell they were related because their faces were so similar.

The stern-faced father was built like a guy who did construction for a living.

The son was something else entirely. He had to be 6-foot three. Maybe four. Five? He was massively obese in an age where the fat kid was still an aberration—you were only allowed one per classroom or neighborhood and it was usually the kid who came from money. This guy was *big* big. 300 pounds. Maybe more.

But more important than anything else, he looked to be about my age, and when you don't have any friends, you don't tend to discriminate as much when a candidate presents himself.

I switched the stereo off, hoisted Gene up, transferred him to a hip and went outside to introduce myself. As I approached, I gave this new kid the once-over.

He didn't seem to have any idea how big he was. He wore his hair slicked into a classic 50s pompadour when dry hair for youth was the rage. On the surface, he appeared pretty damned intimidating, but he acted serenely cool. I detected a slight scowl, but something told me he was okay.

"You movin' in?" I asked as I sidled up.

"Yep," without looking at me.

"Man, that's a big trailer."

He continued not looking at me. "80 feet."

I picked up on a slight southern drawl. He definitely wasn't from the north. I sized him up and threw out an offer. "You like pizza?"

He slowly turned his head and made eye contact. His grimace dissipated and a smile crept its way across his pudgy face. He didn't have to say a word. It was all done with telepathy.

He liked pizza alright.

We went to Steve Oreno's after Dorothy came home to relieve me.

On the walk over, I found out he was a year older than me, but we were in the same grade. He was pretty agile for his size. Didn't have any problem keeping up with my pace. No heavy breathing.

I took a stab at bonding. "Hey, I never asked you what your name is."

"Darrell. How about you?"

"Tim."

"It's a pleasure to meet you, Tim," he said with manners.

Conversely, my manners were not on display as I stared at his Brylcreemed head and he called me on it.

He stopped. "What?"

"Anybody ever tell you you look like Elvis?"

He chortled. "No, I don't think I can say that's ever happened."

"No, you do," I observed.

He shook his head and we started walking again. "Fuck you," he deadpanned.

The situation was improving every minute. We'd broken off into f-word territory and that was important to get the formalities out of the way.

"It's the hair. You're Elvis, man," I insisted.

He chuckled at his christening. "Well, I guess there's worse things."

I never meant it as a slam and he sensed that. Even though my heart was with The Beatles, Elvis excited me, too. I was a big fan of the King's movies—even his worst ones— and usually came home from a matinee wanting to work out what I could remember in front of my bedroom mirror. There were no videos or movie channels, so anything we couldn't remember exactly was filled in with imagination and made-up substitute lyrics.

As teenagers, we were kind of left on our own creatively. Parents that nurtured the rock and roll in their kids' souls were rare. Most times, it was a wise move to keep your urges close to your vest.

For somebody who'd only had his new name for 15 minutes, he adjusted on his feet. He didn't seem to mind at all.

Without acknowledging it, I think Elvis thought it was pretty cool.

Steve got to work on our order right away—a *large* pepperoni with *extra* sauce and *extra* cheese—a new indulgence for me, one I would probably never think I was worthy of, but Elvis was treating. We sipped Cokes, seated at the table closest to the jukebox. I led things off by putting the first quarter in. The third time *The Ballad of John and Yoko* kicked in, Elvis laughed.

"So how many times you gonna listen to this song?" he chided.

We chowed down as the record boomed its way through another three plays. Elvis didn't hog the pizza. We split it right down the middle. I got a fair shake even though Elvis had paid for everything but the spins on the jukebox. He had lots of ones in his pocket and didn't seem to mind ponying up when it was time to pay. He was exceedingly generous and I understood that about him from day one.

He saw me eye his wad of bills as he stuffed it back in his shirt pocket.

He offered an explanation without me asking. "My dad doesn't cook."

Steve came out from the back with a broom and swept up a little.

The music stopped. I stood up and put another quarter in.

Elvis grimaced through a mouthful of half-chewed pizza. "You're not gonna play it again, are you?"

Steve leaned the broom up against the counter and applauded his new customer. "Thank God there's finally a voice of reason in the room."

My finger was poised to punch in the letter-number combination for my favorite song. I pulled back and said, "Okay. Here you go," at which point, I punched in some codes that reflected my recently expanded horizons courtesy of Mr. Oreno.

Green River kicked in. CCR struck a chord in the room right from the opening riff.

When Stevie Wonder's *My Cherie Amour* started, Steve Oreno sang along in front of us as if he were a crooner on stage. He swayed loosely with the music and he knew all the words by heart. When it finished, I could have sworn there were tears in his eyes.

When Sly and the Family Stone's *Everyday People* came on, Elvis jumped up and all three of us did this half-assed wiggle in the center of the room while Steve sang into his impromptu microphone broom handle.

It was one of those rare magical moments that lent itself to letting loose. We didn't care how stupid we looked. Allowing myself to feel good was a new experience for me.

Nobody at Steve Oreno's punched you or called you a queer.

Elvis and I strolled back to the mobile home court after diverting to a convenience store where he purchased an orange Popsicle. He'd expertly snapped the two halves apart so we each got one.

We took our time. Did some bullshittin'. Walked lazy.

He asked me the same question Steve Oreno had asked me.

"So why don't you just buy the record?"

"My mother won't let me have it because it has the word 'Christ' in it."

Elvis was a free spirit from the get-go. "Fuck her, man. You just gotta be a little more clever. Hell, I'll even *buy* you the fuckin' thing and you can keep it at my house."

I weighed his offer in silence. I debated myself on whether I had any stones or not.

We neared my trailer. The windows were open because it didn't have air-conditioning like other places. My mother was home and in full Madame Butterfly swing. She sometimes listened to other operas and I wondered why she didn't murder Tosca. Mix it up a little. But she had a fixation about acting out Madame B.

We stopped and stared at my tin can of a home.

Elvis scrunched up his face at her caterwauling. "What the hell is *that*?"

"It's my mother."

Elvis snickered. "Your dad must be fuckin' deaf or somethin' to put up with that."

I looked down and muttered, "My dad's dead." Since the 5th grade, bullies had picked on me because I didn't have a dad—like it was my fault he ran off with another woman and abandoned me. I never understood why kids held you responsible for your parents' complications. Making that admission to a brand new friend was risky. But even though I'd known him for less than a day, I felt an instant kinship with Elvis. I could trust him not to be mean.

Elvis didn't press for details. He looked down at me and shrugged offhandedly. "Yeah, my mom's dead."

It made us equal in a way. We both understood what having only one parent meant. Things were what they were and that was that. He never brought my dead father up again. And I never asked him about his mother.

My mother went for a high note and screeched like fingernails on a chalkboard. She knew she'd botched it, too. "God*damn*it!" we heard her chastise herself.

We knew better than to get closer and moved on. Elvis shook his head.

"Jesus Christ, man. I feel sorry for you."

The Devil's Playthings

Once Elvis made his offer, I didn't wait long to pick the forbidden fruit. I'd get inside my closet and fetal up with a book-sized speaker pressed close against each side of my head. "Christ, you know it ain't easy," indeed.

I wore that record out.

Steve Oreno surprised us one afternoon with a new product he'd acquired—MetBrew near beer—a non-alcoholic beverage that made us imagine we were high. Elvis and I both became instantly addicted and got nervous when Steve got down to his last case. So he ordered more.

This new "beer"-infused tough-guy image perfectly suited us branching out musically. We made that old Seeburg crank the Steppenwolf. *Born to Be Wild. Magic Carpet Ride. Sookie Sookie.*

We shared packs of cigarettes. Sometimes we each had our own. We weren't too particular about brands. Most places still had lobbies with cigarette machines. Or you could steal them from supermarkets and convenience stores.

Occasionally, Steve let us smoke, but only at the outside tables. No adults ever came to Steve Oreno's so he was safe from parental supervision. His business was driven by the forces of youth.

We spent many an afternoon wolfing down Steve's killer pizza. We cleared our palates by sucking down cans of MetBrew accompanied by the occasional cigarette.

It was all so very grown-up.

Elvis and I spent hours quietly reading in his living room. He ran the air-conditioning non-stop. We'd lie side by side underneath the vent.

We read DC comics. Elvis had a stack of them in his bottom bureau drawer. *Superman. Batman. World's Finest* was great because it combined both of our favorite guys with capes in the same stories.

But our favorite periodical was Forrest J Ackerman's *Famous Monsters of Filmland* magazine. Forrest had devoted his life to the preservation of all things Sci-Fi to include most monster movies made up through the mid-60s. He steered clear of gore and concentrated on the classics. Frankenstein. Dracula. The Wolfman and the Mummy. The Hunchback of Notre Dame and the Phantom of the Opera. He gave us an insight into the humanity of the deformed. There was always sympathy for the monster. Kids my age ate it up because we were deformed too, only inside where you couldn't see it.

We pored over black and white pictures of our mentor's glorious Ackermansion in sunny southern California. To us, the outside resembled a small castle. The inside rooms were floor-to-ceiling exhibits engineered to boggle a young man's mind—everything from the oil paintings used for his magazine covers to one of Bela Lugosi's original Dracula capes. Forrest said his fans had an open invitation to come out and see the place in person, but the thought of making it 3,000 miles from Maine to California was almost beyond wasting our time.

I studied a picture of Mr. Ackerman. "I wanna meet Forrey some day."

Elvis sneered. He hated it when I called Forrest Forrey even though Mr. Ackerman often referred to himself with that very nickname.

"So you wanna meet him? You fuckin' dink. How you gonna arrange that?"

"I don't know," I said, lost in the fantasy. "But I wanna meet him. I wanna go to the Ackermansion."

Elvis closed the issue he was reading and picked up another one. "Yeah, alright. Well, I wouldn't hold my breath, okay?"

I went from zero to 10 in no time and got into one of my don't-include-me-in-your-loser's-circle attitudes. "No, fuck you, man. I'm gonna meet him some day."

Elvis stared at me and relaxed his face a bit.

"Well...maybe you will," he said as he respectfully placed the *Famous Monsters* he was fanning through back on the small stack I'd brought over.

He stood up and stretched. "What we need is some real magazines."

"Like what?" I asked.

He pointed to the *FM*s. "I mean, this is cool, but…we need some *Playboy*s."

A hush fell over the room.

"How we gonna get those?" I wanted to know.

"The same way you got these *FM*s. Kife 'em."

I morphed into a sitting position. "I don't steal… anymore. Not since I got my paper route."

Elvis puffed up. "What are you talking about? We steal stuff all the time."

I stiffened. "That's cigarettes. That's different."

Elvis got serious. "But *Playboy*'s worth stealing. It's educational."

I tried to reason with him. "I don't know, man. Maybe we should pay for things."

Elvis reasoned right back. "But they ain't gonna sell us a *Playboy*."

True. I tried another tactic. "Does your dad have any?"

"Naw. I looked. He's got a dirty book. That's about it."

I felt the twinge of a spontaneous boner. "He does?"

Elvis dismissed me with a wave. "Yeah. But they're stories. No pictures."

All at once, it seemed hot in the room. I felt like fainting. "You're kidding, right?"

Elvis headed for his father's bedroom. He stopped before he went in and motioned for me to follow. I was nervous as a cat, but I jumped up and did as instructed. I was about to get one of the keys to the kingdom. Take me to your leader.

"What if your dad comes home?"

"Nah. He won't be home for hours."

I watched from the bedroom door as Elvis opened his dad's top dresser drawer and felt under the socks in the back. He hit paydirt and pulled out a paperback he tossed to me.

I studied the cover—solid red with white letters spelling out nothing but the title: *Overtime*.

"Check it out," Elvis said impassively.

I couldn't get it open fast enough. This was an important find, akin to Columbus bumping into the New World. I flipped the cover open and turned to the first page—a mini-table of contents. "There's three different stories in here." This was too good to be true. Three complete sexual adventures!

My eyes were wide with wonder. In front of me was an education that beat any health courses they were teaching in middle school. Words I'd never seen before leapt off the page and poked me aggressively in both eyes. Spunk. Cunny. I wasn't sure what they meant, but I was intrigued.

Elvis took notice of my keen interest. "Pretty good, huh?"

I was hypnotized. "I'll say."

Sonofabitch, Elvis.

He'd been holding out on me.

I made a significant discovery that night. The *Overtime* paperback was so stimulating, I had a continuous erection. My mother knocked on my bedroom door to ask if I was going to eat anything. She'd made some soup. I told her I wasn't feeling well, but truth be told, I couldn't make my boner go away.

I had never masturbated in my life. During a brief stint in the Boy Scouts, I'd been given a Scout handbook to read and way in the back was this section titled "From Boy to Man." It described changes your body went through when entering puberty—the growth of facial and genital hair. Tufts under your arms. Perspiring and the need for deodorant.

The handbook also mentioned wet dreams. Although I'd never had one, I was quite interested in the concept.

I slipped into the bathroom, locked the door, and drew a bath. I would've taken a shower, but we didn't have one. I eased down into the warm water with my now aching-to-be-relieved hard-on. Closing my eyes, I visualized scenes in *Overtime* and rubbed my penis for a minute or two. The most incredible buildup started at the base of my spine and worked its way between my legs and up through my dick.

When the white stuff spurted out into the soapy water, I was stunned. I'd never seen semen before, let alone coming out of my own dick.

The thought was not wasted on me that this was epic.

There was a look my mother got that was unmistakable. It was always alcohol-infused. Her eyes narrowed into black holes. Like she was suspicious. Judging my every nuance. I resented the hell out of this. Her musings were drenched in hypocrisy, so I held everything she said up to the light. But even though I was hip to her patterns, I can't deny she was scary.

Especially on this night.

With an iron-fisted grip on her glass, she white-knuckled on her recliner arms to move herself up in the chair, ice clinking frantically in what was left of her rotgut vodka. Her eyes hardened into slits.

"There's something wrong with you."

The modulation in her voice was always the spooky part. She was never the master of control, so when she spoke in controlled tones, I knew I had to be wary.

I resented having to buckle to her and I'm sure my insolence showed.

She leaned further forward, right on the edge of her seat. "If you don't stop what you're doing, I'm going to take you to a psychiatrist and have a part of your brain cut out."

These ideas of hers always seemed to come out of left field.

"What am I doing that I'm supposed to stop doing?"

Her eyes tightened down on me even more. "You know."

God, she was fucking crazy. "Actually, I don't."

She slid back into the comfort of her chair, took a drink and smiled. "Remember when I used to catch you sleep-walking? Maybe I should have had your brain operated on then. So, is that what you want?"

When she devolved into this unreachable state, she spoke to me as if I was tuned in to her wavelength. I wasn't.

"What are you talking about?"

"Is that what you want? To have a part of your brain cut out?" Her lips curled into a thin cruel smile. "I'll do it. Believe me. I'll do it if you don't stop."

I knew she was dangerous. There was no answer to this insanity. I held my tongue.

She didn't.

"Is that what you want?"

Easy Rider

In the muggy swelter of July, our local one-screen theater hosted Peter Fonda, Dennis Hopper and Jack Nicholson in a movie that grabbed me straight away by the short and curlies. Let's say it opened windows in my mind and I'll leave it at that. The picture was R-rated. You had to be 16. I was *almost* 14 and I didn't even look that. But, small town, small audiences. We reasoned they needed the money and would probably relax the scrutiny. But you never knew.

Elvis saw me freeze up—locked in on the R-rating card in the ticket booth window. He dragged me forward. "They ain't gonna care."

"Easy for you to say." I pointed out, "You look older."

"Well, we need to try," Elvis declared.

I had to agree. That poster out front depicting Captain America with the flag on his back was calling me.

Elvis stepped up to the ticket booth and bought a ticket no problem. But when he moved out of the way and I held my money up to the window, the shrunken old lady in the glass booth gave me a good once-over and furrowed her brow.

"You got any ID?" she asked as she peered over her glasses to get a better look at me.

Elvis stepped back into the picture and tried to smooth things over.

"He's with me."

Maybe she was intimidated by his size, I don't know, but that was it.

She backed off and sold me the ticket.

We were transfixed.

We knew about *Born to Be Wild* from Steve Oreno's, but when we heard those opening staccato guitar licks from *The Pusher*, we were entering a whole new world. I had never seen a movie with sex, drugs, and rock 'n' roll presented as a package. For me, it was a Christmas morning feeling that mostly registered in my lower regions. This movie had everything as far as I was concerned.

This was too damned exciting.

We walked home in the dark.

I was still buzzing. "That was incredible!"

Elvis wasn't totally convinced. "I didn't like the ending."

"Fuck you," I countered eloquently.

He wasn't going to let this die. "No, really. What kind of ending was that? Everything's going along fine and then—"

"You just don't get it."

"Alright. What the fuck did it mean? They're ridin' along and then boom. Like they couldn't figure out how to end it, so they just killed everybody."

I shook my head. "You didn't get it."

Elvis refused to back down. "Explain it to me, dink."

I couldn't really explain it to him, but I knew it meant something.

My desire to read often led me to our local public library. Elvis was a late riser on the weekends, so Saturday mornings were prime time for me.

There was a hush effect when entering libraries. People weren't allowed to talk out loud and strict librarians thought nothing of putting you in your place if they caught you flapping your jaw. There was respect for quiet. If somebody dropped a pin, everybody heard it. For me, that serenity was a lifeline. I spent many an hour escaping in a leather chair at the remote end of a book corridor.

On one of my safe and peaceful mornings, while passing by a section of dictionaries, I took notice of one in particular: *The Dictionary of Slang and Unconventional English*. I had no idea what was in this massive volume, but I was instantly intrigued.

I had to stifle my laughter quite a few times. Hand over mouth stifling. This book was hilarious. There were *pages* devoted to all the ways you could use "fuck" not to mention all the other words you couldn't say on television.

My brain absorbed like a sponge.

I was getting into this jerking off thing. So it was inevitable I would get caught. You just don't want it to be your mother that walks in on you. But she did.

She freaked. "Holy Mary Mother of God, what the hell are you doing?!"

I didn't think it needed an explanation, but I was deeply embarrassed nevertheless.

She slammed the door shut and threatened from the other side, "You and I will talk about this later!"

I dreaded the meeting.

I sat at an angle on the end of the couch closest to her broken-in recliner, staring down into my lap.

She focused on her drink without looking at me. "So…"

I'd rather take a beating. Just get it over with.

"This thing you're doing—" She stopped, reorganized her thoughts. "I guess you're getting too many ideas from these rock and roll musicians. Is that what it is?"

"That has nothing to do with anything."

"Oh, I think it does. Well, just remember, this is how perverts—how perversion—gets going."

As our pow-wow progressed, she got even more sauced on bargain-basement whiskey. Conditions were perfect for her to impart her wisdom about the facts of life. I wasn't sure I wanted to hear this information through her filter, but my mind was pinging like a pinball machine. I must admit I was a tad curious about gaining some new insight now that I was getting a handle on the masturbation deal.

I should have known better with my mother. She had no intention of helping me out.

She poured a fresh belt, took a healthy slug, and burped—not a loud burp where you're just letting pent-up air out—more like a low guttural burp indicating she might heave if she wasn't careful. It was backing up in her throat and she had to pause and re-swallow it. Once she got a grip on herself, she looked over at me.

"Okay. Let's talk about the birds and the bees," she started out.

We heard that expression a lot when I was young. The birds and the bees. Like, what the fuck did that mean? Give me something concrete—a detail I can use.

This was not to be.

"When you get older," she continued, "you'll fall in love and then…"

Mentally I was all ears. And then *what*?

"You'll get married…and turn out the lights."

And?

"And so…someday that'll happen."

What? *What* will happen?

"So wait until you're in love," she trailed off.

Fuck! I wanted to scream in her face. That's *it?* That's all you got?

Tears streamed out of her eyes. Christ. The crying drunk shit. Couldn't we get through anything without descending into melancholy?

She wasn't done. "Sorry I had to be the one to tell you about sex, but I'm doing the best I can," she apologized. I wanted to run from the room. I'd rather learn it on the street.

But wait. There was more. There weren't too many three-sheets-to-the-wind crying jags we could get through without bringing up my dead father. He was *dead*, okay? I'd never known him. He'd left by the time I was four. On the surface, I was fine not knowing what I'd missed. But she could never let it die. Her hate had to spew and I resented her personalizing it for me.

Cue the punch line. "I wish your sonofabitchin' father was here to do this. I shouldn't have to be the one telling you about growing into a man."

She splashed another finger or two into her glass and wrapped up the character assassination. "The reason he left me is because he never liked you. He was never interested in being a part of your life."

I was well past reacting to these assaults. I sat stone-faced.

"I love you, Timmy," she lied. "But your father, no good sonofabitch that he was, didn't want you around." She subdued a belch. "He hated your guts, Timmy."

She reached into her too-loose Muumuu house dress and pulled a well-used Kleenex from her bra. She used the rumpled ball of soft paper to dab under her eyes and wiped the clear mucus collecting on her upper lip.

She righted herself in her seat. "Well, you need to know these things," she decreed as she waved a dismissive hand. The show was over. She didn't need a punching bag anymore.

I got up quietly and padded down the hallway to my bedroom.

I shut the door and fell face-first on top of my covers with all my clothes on. Rolling over, I stared at the ceiling and thought about how fucked up life was.

I fell asleep thinking about how much my father hated my guts.

Neil Armstrong

On the morning of July 21st, the front page of the papers I delivered boasted a black and white photo of the first man ever to walk on the moon. Neil Armstrong. The Eagle had landed the previous night and just hours before cutting the bundle on my newspapers, I'd watched old Neil take the first step for mankind onto the lunar surface. Even my mother was respectful and kept her mouth shut.

Before he'd been shot dead when I was in second grade, President Kennedy mandated we'd walk on the moon by the end of the 60s, and by God, we did. On that particular day, I didn't care if people paid for their papers or not, I was just happy to deliver the news of our mutual accomplishment.

I was proud of my country and I didn't even understand what that meant.

At the donut shop, the woman behind the counter asked excitedly, "Did you watch it on TV?"

"Yes, Ma'am, I did," I beamed.

"That was somethin' else, wasn't it?"

She reached behind the counter and pulled out a fresh delicacy and placed it in my upturned palm.

"Thanks," I said with genuine gratitude.

I turned to leave and she saw the flag sewn on my back. An instant frost blanketed the room. After watching Peter Fonda in *Easy Rider*, I was determined to match his cool. I'd kicked off that transformation by acquiring and hand-stitching one of those little cloth flags they stick on veterans' graves to the back of a black t-shirt.

She alerted. "Hey."

I didn't like the way she said it. I rotated slowly to face her, brushing cinnamon sugar dust from my bottom lip.

She leveled her eyes at me to great effect. "Don't ever come in here wearing that again."

I maintained a poker-face as much as I could and made tracks. On the verge of tears, I pedaled off on my bike. It was never my intention to offend anyone. I just wanted to look cool. And what was wrong with thinking the American flag looked cool sewn on my back?

To the people at the donut shop, I was just the paperboy. They'd never asked me what my name was, so why was I worried about whether they liked me or not? Simple. Because at that age, I did. I worried about everybody liking me, and when they didn't, I was disappointed on so many levels.

That afternoon, Elvis and I made our way to Steve Oreno's. Steve clunked a couple of bottles of Coke on the counter and uncapped them before going in the back to start our pizza. After he disappeared, Elvis and I stood over the Seeburg and punched in selections.

We sat down. The music kicked in. We sipped our sodas.

Steve came out with our large pepperoni, and as he set it down, he caught a glimpse of the back of my shirt.

"Hey." He said it in the same tone of voice the donut shop woman had used.

Elvis and I both looked up at the hulking Italian hovering over us.

"What the fuck is that on the back of your shirt?" Steve demanded. He was extremely tense.

It was uncomfortable. I was instantly surrounded, smothered by a constricting cloud of bad.

"It's a flag," I heard myself answer way too casually for the situation.

"Yeah, I can see that."

I waited for the hammer to fall.

Steve wiped his hands in disgust. "Eat and go."

With that, he went back behind the counter and wiped up surfaces he'd already cleaned. He slammed some pans around. And I felt like a piece of shit for being a disappointment, even though it wasn't intentional. It would have been better if he'd said "I saw too many of my friends sacrifice their lives for that flag. Don't ever come in here again with that on."

But he didn't. He flung his rag onto the counter and pointed at me. "You heard me. Eat and go." He went into the back, robbing me of any opportunity to apologize.

I choked.

Elvis continued eating, unaffected.

"C'mon, let's go," I croaked as I got up.

Elvis didn't budge. "You can go. I'm fuckin' hungry."

I gave him the what-the-fuck salute. "No, c'mon, let's go. He's pissed."

Elvis laughed and wiped his chin with a napkin. "He's pissed at you, not me."

Hey, thanks for the solidarity. "Alright, fuck off."

Elvis shook his head at me like I was an idiot and chomped down on a big bite of crust as I evaporated out the door.

The best speeches are always made on the way home. It occurred to me on the journey back to my trailer how insulted I was that no one except Elvis seemed to get the coolness of my artistic expression. And even then he hadn't supported me in the clinch. Fuck. I wasn't trying to make any anti-American statement.

I just wanted to be special to someone.

When I got home, there was a Cadillac convertible parked in our driveway. Someone was visiting. I heard laughter through an open window.

I went up the 3 metal stairs and tried our door. Locked. Our doors were never locked until bedtime and sometimes not even then. I wiggled the handle. Nothing. I rapped and heard my mother tell me to hold on as she unlocked the door from inside.

She pushed the door open and backed up so I could enter. "Oh, hello, Timmy," she said in the voice she used when she was being phony and trying to impress someone. She was dolled up. Lipstick. Her best dress. High-heeled shoes.

On the couch sat a man I'd never seen before. Bill. He looked to be my mother's age. You could tell he was all macho—he sported a tightly trimmed flat-top—no Beatle haircut for him. He wore a crisply ironed white button-down long-sleeved shirt open at the collar. Even with the shirt, there was no hiding his manly physique. He had thick arms and a barrel-chest. The bright white of the shirt contrasted handsomely with a deeply etched farmer's tan.

My mother stood off to one side without making any introductions. Bill got up to shake my hand, man-to-man. He wasn't super-tall, but he was powerfully muscular. He squeezed my hand so firmly, I thought he might fuck up my knuckles. He flashed a million-dollar smile. His teeth were white-white and perfect. He seemed friendly enough. But with a weird glint in his eye. And he had a wedding ring on.

"Timmy, I've heard a lot about you. It's nice to finally meet you."

At least he had manners.

He released his iron-grip and sat back down. My mother drifted to her recliner and settled on the edge of it. On her best behavior.

I looked down and noticed mixed drinks on the coffee table.

They stared at me staring at the drinks. I knew something was wrong with the picture, but I had no interest in trying to figure out what was going on. I had my own problems.

"Nice to meet you," I murmured as I skulked away to my room.

Bill offered up a friendly half-wave as I exited and out of the corner of my eye, I saw his smile change to a confused expression. It never dawned on me he'd caught sight of the flag sewn on the back of my t-shirt.

I closed myself inside my room and listened at the paper-thin door.

"They'll be some new rules," I heard Bill dictate. "He needs a decent haircut for one."

I waited for my mother to come to my defense.

"Sure. Whatever you want to do," she demurred.

A feeling of dread washed over me. My mother wasn't good with relationships, so what did this guy see in her? Where did he even come from? Not that I felt I deserved an answer. Most adults I knew had no interest in hanging out with kids. We were beneath them.

My mother's track record with men blew.

I had no reason to think she wouldn't fuck this up, too.

Alcohol

I got up before it was light and dressed in silence. When I tip-toed out of my room, I heard snoring. Snoring plural. My mother's door was closed.

The back door of the trailer was right off the entrance to my room. I cracked it open and peeked outside.

The Cadillac was still there.

I couldn't get focused delivering papers that morning.

Eat and go.

Steve's words rang out in my head over and over, like some Chinese water torture on steroids. I'd fucked up in the eyes of someone I respected and all at once I felt responsibility about actions having consequences. It didn't feel good to be disapproved of by someone I emulated. Even at 13, I got the import of all three syllables he'd uttered. Needless to say, I never wore that shirt into his place again, although I'd have it on when riding the Wonder Bike, imagining a motorcycle thundering underneath me.

On my way back from my paper route that morning, two old geezers in a pickup pulled up alongside me. Exactly like in *Easy Rider*. And just like in the movie, the one on the passenger side leaned out his window as they passed by. "Hey, you sonofabitch, get the goddamned flag off your back!"

And Elvis thought the ending of *Easy Rider* was bullshit.

They sped off. Good thing. They made me nervous.

Well, at least they didn't act out the *entire* last scene of the movie and blow me away with a shotgun.

When I skidded into my driveway, the Cadillac was gone.

I threw my bike down and went inside.

My mother was up, sipping on a morning screwdriver. She sat at our chintzy dinette table in our cramped kitchen decked out in a ratty bathrobe that was half-pulled shut. Her hair was a mess. Make-up smeared. It was quite a contrast from her presentation the previous evening.

She didn't say anything at first. Not even good morning. She slurped on her drink and watched me pull a box of Cap'n Crunch out from underneath the sink. The box was almost empty, but there was enough for a small bowl.

My mother didn't cook much, so a lot of my early nutrition came out of boxes and cans. Any dream of having a real breakfast was just that—a dream. There were never eggs or pancakes or French toast. Only people on TV ate bacon and waffles with butter and syrup.

I checked the fridge. Wow. There was orange juice and it appeared we almost had enough milk for my cereal. I shook what cereal was left in the box into a bowl I retrieved out of the dish strainer to the right of the stainless steel sink. I added a little water from the tap to supplement the milk. I set my meal down on the kitchen counter, grabbed a clean glass from a cabinet, and reached into the refrigerator to get out the OJ.

"You can't have that," she said to my back.

I'd forgotten. Temporary insanity. Mustn't pilfer from her supplies. In our house, if we had orange juice, it was never a fruit drink, it was a mixer. It got under my skin. Most of the time, I could put up with her shit, but every once in a while, my hormones raged and I did something to invite trouble. Usually it was talking back. It made her crazy when I went out on a limb and poked at her.

I went to put the juice back in the fridge.

"You can't have that," she repeated as I opened the door.

God, she couldn't let things die sometimes. "I know. You already told me."

"I need it for work," she rationalized.

I'd already returned the carton unmolested. But I couldn't keep my jackass mouth shut. "I *got* what you said, okay?"

I don't think she had any idea how disgusted I was with her getting fucked up before she went to work. Her reasoning was that she needed to level out and nobody could smell vodka on her breath. My reasoning was: You're a fuckin' *nurse*, for Chrissakes. Can't you show some responsibility to the human race?

My mother didn't like back talk. Especially when her brain was pickled. That made her extra-sensitive.

"I deserve to drink," she said under her breath as she took another gulp.

I didn't even want to sit at the same table with her, so I stood to eat. I leaned the small of my back against the edge of the kitchen counter as I munched through my bowl of cereal. The more I looked down at her pathetic state, the more I resented her.

"So where'd you meet Bill?" I asked nonchalantly.

"AA," she replied as she took another sip.

I flashed on the mixed drinks I'd seen on the coffee table the previous day. "AA?" I hurled fuel on the fire. "Weren't you guys *drinking*?"

My mother reacted with great hostility to observations of the obvious from the peanut gallery.

"That's none of your business," she snarled.

Sure it was, I thought to myself. You're introducing this motherfucker into our lives. Yeah, it matters.

I didn't let it die. "If he's going to AA, why is he drinking?"

Without looking up at me, she laughed softly into her next sip and said, "He cheats."

Like that was a good thing. As if we didn't have enough problems, now we were going to introduce another drunk into our lives. I couldn't believe it. I despised her with every inch of my being.

"Great, this is all we need," I heard myself say under my breath. Within a split-second, she was up out of her chair and on me, flailing away. I held my arms up, crossed in front of my face so she wouldn't poke an eye out.

She backed up. Seething. Hating me even more than I hated her. She had Moosie eyes. "Your father was right to leave," she spat. "I believed, but he saw right through you. You'd better straighten up and fly right or you'll end up a bum just like him."

I unleashed without reservation. "Hey, you know what? Fuck *you*. You've never amounted to a goddamned thing your whole life, so don't lecture me on what to fuckin' do, okay?"

I might as well have slapped her. Maybe it would have been better if I had. At least I would've gotten my lick in.

I didn't see her retort coming and her hand made a solid connection, right along the nerve bundle on my jaw line. I saw stars.

And then I saw red.

I guess I grabbed her. I don't know. If I did, it was instinctive. Somehow she ended up thrown back into her chair.

She uncrinkled herself and hissed at me. "How dare you raise a hand to me. How *dare* you."

It was the first time I realized she no longer had power over me physically. The point wasn't lost on her either.

"How *dare* you," she repeated boldly, but she spoke in a treble tinged with a nervous awareness.

I stood my ground.

She wisely kept her seat at the table.

There was a new sheriff in town.

Elvis and I spent the day reading *Famous Monsters of Filmland* with some *Creepy* and *Eerie* thrown in. Silence and respect for the reading experience was paramount. During reading hours, we treated Elvis's living room like a library. The only sounds were the turning of pages and the lighting and smoking of cigarettes.

It didn't matter how many times we'd read the magazines, we enjoyed each trip through an issue. I was lost in the ad section of an *FMOF* when Elvis got up and walked off into his room.

He returned carrying a shoebox. "Got something for ya," he said as he handed it to me.

It was heavy. I removed the lid and my jaw dropped.

"I figured you could make better use of them than me."

The box was jam-packed with Beatles bubble gum cards. Hundreds of them. My mouth hung open. "Are you kidding?"

"Nope," he grinned. "They're all yours."

I was speechless. I was touched by his thoughtfulness and he knew it without me saying a word.

"I just bought them for the gum," Elvis reassured me. "I never gave a shit about the cards."

Well, I gave a shit.

My mother came upon me and my treasure that night. I had my cards spread around me on the bed—all 624 of them.

She went to frosty in an instant. "Where did you get these?"

"From Darrell."

She shifted into accusatory. "He didn't just *give* you these."

"Yeah, he did."

God, I fucking hated her. She could never conceive of someone giving you something just because they liked you. And no wonder. She'd fucked so many people over in her travels, it wasn't funny.

"Why would he do that?" she pressed.

"Because he's my friend, that's why."

"Bullshit."

And then she gave up. She left it at that. It was odd what things she decided to pick at and what she chose to ignore.

As long as she left me alone, that's all I cared about.

Dorothy befriended Elvis early on after seeing him walking around with me. Maybe in her eyes, he had potential as a backup babysitter, I don't know. If that was the case, I wanted to tell her she'd never have need of a backup, because when it came to her, I was *always* available.

Summer evenings could be warm and muggy, but the temperature often cooled after dark because we were so close to the ocean. Sometimes Dorothy invited us in to listen to records. We usually didn't talk during a song. Dorothy was as much of a musical professor to us as Steve Oreno was. Their tastes were similar in that they both liked what we liked, but they were tuned into a whole lot of other things we'd never heard before and we were digging the exposure, absorbing every morsel.

It wasn't lost on Elvis and me that Steve and Dorothy were adults we admired who respected us despite our age difference. They understood that we were still learning. And secretly, I think it delighted them to share new things with an appreciative audience. Everyone enjoys having their knowledge acknowledged.

One night, after putting Gene down, Dorothy lit up a cigarette, turned down the lights, and spun up some soul. We borrowed Dorothy's lighter and fired up as well. It was understood that if she was smoking, it was okay for us to do it, too. We didn't have to ask permission anymore. In seconds, the whole top half of the room was a cloud of blue haze, which totally added to the forbidden effect.

Dorothy was in a very up mood and she started off with The Friends of Distinction. *Grazing in the Grass.* Steve had this ditty in the Seeburg, but we'd never played it. It was upbeat with lots of peppy horns. Dorothy grooved it out. She laughed and sang along with abandon. I've loved that song ever since.

The tune ended and she swapped out vinyl.

She wore tight shorts and she looked good in them, her bare legs flawless. Her blouse was probably open one button too many—at least as far as adolescent boys were concerned. She didn't bend over provocatively when she put records on, it was just *all* provocative to us. She could have stood like a statue for hours on end and we would have been content to sit and stare at her and smoke cigarettes.

The music started up. She slow-danced in bare feet, swaying back and forth to Percy Sledge's *When a Man Loves a Woman.*

God, she was sexy as hell. Elvis stared like he didn't care if he got caught—he had a huge crush on her from the get-go. I was so smitten that I had to avert my gaze occasionally because it was too intense when we locked eyes, especially in situations where she was grinding hypnotically a few feet in front of me. It was the way she caressed herself. The way she smiled with her eyes closed, bathing in the afterglow of a previous lover unknown to us. Escaping from her humdrum life in the center of a trailer living room, undulating in front of two horny teenage boys.

The song ended. She removed the needle and put the record back in its sleeve. Dorothy was a little more cavalier with her own possessions than I was—she didn't think anything of handling her records improperly and getting fingerprints all over the surfaces. She picked out another record, but paused before taking it out.

The last few times we'd been over, she'd had a drink or two in front of us. When I first met her, I never saw any evidence of alcohol in her trailer. This was a new thing and it visited with mixed results. The drug's influence either made her happy and relaxed or it made her cry in her beer.

She tripped slightly as she reached over to a half-empty pint of Seagrams whiskey and took a snort straight from the bottle. No question, she was getting liquored up. Not that I wasn't used to seeing that kind of behavior—my mother taught master classes.

Dorothy set the bottle down and subtly swiped one corner of her mouth against the bend of a delicate wrist. She used a thumb and an index finger to pull the next piece of our musical education out of its cardboard sleeve.

Neil Diamond. Once again, something Steve Oreno had already been wise enough to stock in his Seeburg, but Elvis and I refused to listen because we didn't know any better. We were ignorant in the finest sense of the word.

We both looked on dumbly as Dorothy put on *Sweet Caroline*. The vibe was immediate. I loved Neil's voice, I loved the song, and I especially loved his spokesmodel.

She smiled and outstretched both arms, hands giving us the c'mon. "Dance with me," she beckoned.

Elvis and I searched each other for a clue. Nope. Clueless.

"I can't," I demurred.

"You don't know if you don't try," she coaxed. She looked right at me and I still shook my head no. What an idiot.

Elvis was a little more savvy than me. A light bulb came on over his head. She didn't have to ask him twice. The big lug jumped *right* up and gushed, "I'll try!"

All of a sudden, he was Fred Astaire.

Dorothy applauded his bravado. "Alright! A man with confidence!"

Elvis's close proximity to my crush made me *intensely* jealous. I was envious of his boldness. He seemed to reach out and take what he wanted without feeling guilty about it. I was still trying to relax into that concept.

Dorothy worked around him, dipping, weaving suggestively, dangerously close to his waistline. And Elvis *responded*! What the fuck?! Who knew he could even *dance*, let alone steal the fuckin' show! I was livid!

I watched my friend knock the socks off my secret girlfriend and I had to keep it all under wraps. I sat there calmly and smoked my cigarette while Elvis emerged as a future *Soul Train* dancer. I pretended it didn't bother me.

About halfway through the song, I couldn't take it anymore. I reached over, grabbed Dorothy's pint, and took a shot. I wasn't used to liquor and my timing was beautiful. I wolfed the whiskey, Dorothy saw me and wagged a finger. I waved her off like I could handle myself. Don't worry about me. Then all at once, my body registered the poison I had just exposed it to and instinctively went into rejection mode.

I half-cough-sprayed behind a clenched fist. My head turned purple as I tried to quash my reaction to spitting up the rest of the gasoline I'd tossed back like a pro. Thankfully Elvis had his back to me and I was spared the additional embarrassment of him seeing me act badly.

To add insult to injury, Dorothy was enjoying herself and I really resented her having fun without me being a part of it.

I also resented the fact that I'd spurned an open invitation to be a part of the festivities. I'd kicked myself in my own ass.

Dorothy smiled at Elvis approvingly. "You got it, Darrell!"

I attempted to appear unfazed.

Dorothy wasn't a mean person. She gave me another chance. "Come on, Timmy! You can do it!"

She called me Timmy. Dammit. She'd always respected my almost being an adult by calling me Tim. In retrospect, I think she was probably being nothing more than playful. Running someone's suspected intent through your sensitivity filters can be tricky as an adult, let alone as a teenager. I felt like I was invisible.

Elvis got into this sexually charged James Brown groove and Dorothy loved it. "There you go! You're a natural!" she squealed.

She was so beautiful, I was willing to make a fool of myself. I got up to dance. I started out unsteady and stayed pretty stiff. Dorothy tried to loosen me up with encouragement. "You'll get it!" She'd show me an example of what to follow and I'd freeze up completely. She had a funny look on her face like she couldn't figure out why I couldn't just give in.

"Just keep trying!" she tossed over her shoulder as she abandoned me and turned back to synchronize with Elvis.

I was envious of Elvis and not in a healthy way.

But I never told him that.

They Say It's Your Birthday

My mother warned me I was to be available on my birthday. Bill had a surprise for me. Like an idiot, I was dumb enough to believe he was bringing me a meaningful gift. In the days leading up to my special event, I imagined a lot of ridiculous shit. Maybe he was going to give me a ball and glove or a guitar. I was dumb enough to fantasize he might even bring me a fishing rod and then offer to take me fishing.

I should have known my birthday would blow. My mother destroyed all holidays with her drinking and her personality. It was a ritual. We could never enjoy a holiday for long before the atmosphere deteriorated.

I shuffled out to the kitchen around 7 AM.

My mother was already into the juice, into the darting-eyed paranoid part.

"Happy birthday," she said flatly.

Frankly, I was surprised she remembered. I looked in our barren refrigerator and shut the door. I went for a slice of Wonder bread out of the bag on the counter.

"Bill's going to be here at nine," she announced.

"Why?" I asked, revealing a little more concern than I'd wanted to.

"He's going to take you to get a haircut."

"What?"

"He doesn't like the way you look."

"I like the way I look. I don't want to get my hair cut."

"You're going."

"What if I don't want to?"

"You're going."

"He's not my father. You can't make me."

"*He* can."

I censored myself by stuffing the last of the bread into my mouth and walking off to my bedroom. I wanted to scream. I wanted her to stand up for herself and protect me in the process. But she was weak. And I hated her for it.

And in turn, I hated myself for not being something more than I was.

Bill showed promptly at 9 AM reeking of Aqua Velva. He wasted no time getting me into his Caddy for our trip to the barbershop. The first thing I noticed when I got into the cushy leather upholstery on the passenger side was a small cooler filled with iced cans of Schlitz. One of the cans was already open.

The car floated. I'd never ridden in a Cadillac before.

Bill not only sipped freely from his open container, he chose to light up as well. Camels with no filters. This guy was hardcore through and through.

I didn't want to talk, but he goaded me.

"I think you're going to feel better when you get a decent looking haircut. You need to get rid of that mop."

"I like my hair," I said under my breath as I shied away from him.

"Why? 'Cause you want to look like some dirty hippie?"

I didn't take the bait. I wanted to inform this ignoramus that flattops weren't in anymore, but he wasn't interested in a two-way conversation that involved reasoning. Maybe if I was really a man, I would have bummed a cigarette off him. And who knows? He might have handed one over if I'd asked. But I could tell anything I said was only digging a bigger hole for myself.

I clammed up for the most part, but it didn't really matter. The ride was short. We only had one ominous exchange.

He blew out a long cylinder of blue smoke. "You ever raise a hand to your mother?"

"Excuse me?"

His jaw tightened. "You heard me. You ever hit her?"

"No." End of story.

"I heard different."

"The only time I have ever even held my arms up against her was to stop her from hitting me in the face."

He eyed me heavy on that one. "Hmmph."

Bill found a spot right in front of George's Barbershop. As he put the car into park, he turned to me and gave me his movie star smile. "Hey, when you go into a barbershop, remember they cut each other's hair, so you should always pick the one with the worst haircut." He chortled for punctuation.

I couldn't even manage a half-smile, even though on the surface, what he'd imparted appeared to be helpful advice you could use from time to time.

We walked inside and Bill greeted the barbers by name. George was the older gent and Carl was the young hip blond dude. George greeted him back as he cashed a customer out, but Carl only tipped his scissors as he finished trimming the back of some husky fella's neck.

I noticed the haircuts on both George and Carl before we even sat down. They sucked. Both of these guys looked hacked up, but George's cut wasn't nearly as severe. Assessing the situation, I figured I'd take my chances and go for the young guy.

"Next!" old George announced as he shook out the apron and dusted off his chair.

Bill nudged me to get up.

"I don't want him," I whispered.

Bill screwed his face up like I was from outer space.

"You said I could pick which one," I reminded him.

Bill reached over and grabbed hold of my closest elbow, forcing me to a standing position. I got the message. I walked the 4 steps to my fate and sat down.

George was delighted. Another victim. As he finished securing the paper collar around my neck, he angled his head toward Bill and said, "How do we want it cut today?"

Bill beamed. "Short. Summer short."

"Will do," George agreed.

It didn't take him long to do his worst. He even old-schooled it by shaving my neck in the back with a straight razor, then proudly asked me what I thought as he brandished a mirror so I could see the damage reflected in the wall mirror in front of me.

God, I looked like a fucking moron. As out of place as you could be in 1969.

Apparently the trip was solely for my benefit since Bill didn't bother to get himself a trim while he was there. He paid, making sure to include a modest tip. Pleasantries were exchanged and we left.

"See you next time," George offered up cheerily.

Not if I had anything to do with it.

Bill put his arm on my shoulder as we exited, as if we were related. "Now you look like a man instead of a monkey." He was proud of himself. Good deed for the day accomplished.

As we got back into Bill's car, my neck itched with tiny little hairs George had failed to brush off. It was getting hot out. Bill started up the Caddy, but didn't put the windows down. He lit up a smoke, popped another Schlitz, and admired George's handiwork.

We didn't speak on the way home.

I couldn't wait to see what other birthday surprises awaited me.

When we got back, my mother had put out a half-dozen frosted cupcakes with 2-inch white candles—one candle in each of the 6 cupcakes. I didn't really get it since I was turning 14. The numbers didn't match up, but nothing ever did with my mother.

"Your haircut looks terrific," she marveled as she lit a match and warbled *Happy Birthday* while Bill hummed along in the background to her lighting the candles.

"Make a wish," she said all sing-song. I could tell she'd already had a couple of belts.

Yeah, I'll make a fucking wish. I wish all of you were dead. Stone cold in the fuckin' ground. That's what I wish.

She locked eyes with me. "Did you make a wish?"

"Yeah." I just wished it would come true. Right then and there.

"Well, blow out the candles!" she cooed.

There is no God.

I blew them out and not too cleverly.

She handed me a card. I ripped it open. It was pretty generic. She'd written "Love from Mama" in red ink along the borders inside. Mama? I'd never called her Mama in my life.

"And now Bill has something for you I think you're really going to like."

Bill handed a black wallet to me. "I thought this might be something you could use. Sorry, I didn't have time to wrap it."

I opened the wallet up—it was empty. He shook his head and said, "Oh, yeah. You need something to put in that, don't ya?" At which point, he opened his own rather fat wallet and pulled out a fiver. He held it out in front of me before giving it up. "Don't spend it all in one place."

I'll try not to. Fuckweed.

And that was it.

Another holiday memory.

Elvis did a double-take when he saw me. "Jesus Christ, man. You got scalped! What the fuck happened to you?"

I was still in the humiliation stage. "Don't remind me."

He couldn't quit marveling. "Damn. That's a serious fuckin' haircut."

"Tell me about it."

We walked up Steve Oreno's steps and stopped before going in. Elvis looked down at my haircut and shook his head. He couldn't help but laugh. I might have laughed too, but it wasn't pleasant to be a part of the comedy.

Steve was wiping the counter down when we came inside. He took one look and like Elvis, couldn't help but laugh. "Okay. That's very John Wayne."

Elvis surprised me by announcing he was paying for everything because it was my birthday. But it got better than that. Steve piped up. "It's your birthday? Really?"

I nodded my head in acknowledgment.

"On the house," he announced.

And a good time was had by all.

I don't know how Dorothy knew it was my birthday, but she did. We stopped by her place in the afternoon and she invited us in. She'd actually baked a cake and frosted it with vanilla icing. Plus she had the right number of candles.

We'd been sitting in the living room for probably a half hour when she slipped off into the kitchen. A minute or two later, she reappeared carrying her presentation with all the candles lit, singing *Happy Birthday* accompanied by Elvis who managed to carry his weight in the vocals department. The cake was slightly lop-sided, but it was perfect to me. It even had "Happy Birthday, Tim!" scrawled out with blue lines of frosting.

Dorothy set it down on the coffee table. "Okay, make a wish and blow out the candles."

I made a wish. But it wasn't the same wish I'd wished earlier for my mother and Bill. I blew out the candles on the first take and Dorothy leaned over and kissed me on the cheek. "Happy birthday, sweetie."

She hopped up and headed for the kitchen again. "Oh! Almost forgot!" In a flash, she was back with a wrapped package the shape of a record album. It even had a ribbon and a bow on it. And it came with a card. I didn't want to disturb how beautiful it all was.

"Open the card!" she gushed.

I tore the envelope open. Inside was a *Yellow Submarine* card they'd both inscribed. Elvis's said, "Happy Birthday!" and Dorothy's read, "To a really nice guy! Happy Birthday, Tim!"

I picked the package up and shifted it around in my hands. "Okay. Feels like a record."

Dorothy laughed. "Yeah, no kidding."

I made initial attempts at peeling tape off without tearing the paper. I wanted to save it.

"Just rip it off," Dorothy coaxed.

So I did.

"You're always playing mine, so we figured you needed one. We both chipped in."

The White Album by The Beatles. I was so touched, I choked and couldn't completely stifle it. It was enough that Dorothy noticed. She sat next to me on the couch and put a hand on one of my forearms. And that's all she had to do to heal. Then she reached up and ruffled my short spiky hair. I instinctively pulled away.

Dorothy smiled. "What?"

"Don't make fun of my haircut," I said looking down.

"I wasn't," she corrected. "I think it's sexy."

And that's all it took to make me like short hair.

The party was over. Elvis had already gone home. I was about to leave when Dorothy's phone rang. She picked it up and spoke in low, sultry tones, saying her words so soft, I couldn't make them out even though I was sitting 8 feet away.

She hung up and I couldn't resist asking, "Who was that?"

"My boyfriend Peter," she said coolly.

This was the first I'd heard of this. "You have a boyfriend?"

"Yeah, and I really like him, too. Anyway, he's coming over so you gotta go."

So much for healing.

Free Entertainment

Elvis and I trekked down to the annual Lobster Fest in Rockland. We were willing to hoof the 3-mile walk because we'd heard about the carnival atmosphere. Wall-to-wall people. Creaky rides. Food booths. Cheap games of chance. We would also discover we could pick up cigarettes without having to show ID.

We found ourselves at the ring-toss game. The barker shouted right into our faces while I aimed. "C'mon! Try your luck! Shoot till you win! No losers here! Everybody gets a prize! Shoot till you win!"

I tossed a few rings and managed to land one on a spike attached to a carton of cigarettes.

Elvis jumped up and down as much as he could and slapped me on the back.

Paydirt.

They were Newport menthols. Over the next few days, Elvis and I colluded in wooded areas that skirted the trailer park until we'd smoked all 10 packs end to end.

After two days of this destructive behavior, I hacked at home like I'd just stepped off an emphysema ward. My mother was three sheets to the wind, but I was disturbing enough for her to notice.

"My God, are you alright?" she asked with an exasperated tone. Yeah. God forbid she might have to take me to the doctor.

"Yeah, I'm fine," I croaked.

Mother was slipping into darkness, so the timing was good for me.

There were no follow-up questions.

Dorothy disappeared for three days. On the second day, I spotted a battered pick-up truck in her driveway. I went over and knocked.

The door was opened by a tall gangly guy in his late 20s with oily combed over hair. High and tight over the ears. He was comical looking. Big Dennis the Menace cowlick. Buddy Holly glasses with dirt specks and smudged fingerprints. He burst into a toothy grin. "Well, who are you?"

"I'm—I'm Tim," I stammered.

He thrust out a welcoming hand. "I'm Jim. Nice to meet ya," he said as we shook. He waved me through the entrance. "Come on in."

I did as I was told and he pulled the door shut behind me.

The living room was stuffy and silent. I sat down on one end of the couch. Jim went immediately to the kitchen and retrieved a bottle of Coke and two tumblers. He came back in, sat on the edge of the recliner, and without asking, poured two ice-cold refreshments.

We picked up our glasses and sipped. The carbonation burned my throat.

"Where's Dorothy?" I asked, trying to appear only half-interested.

He straightened up. "I was hoping you could tell me that. I've been looking for her."

I put my Coke down. "Who are you?"

"I'm Dottie's husband."

It took me a moment to collect my thoughts. *Husband?*

He kept his eyes on me. "You know where she's at?"

"Nope."

I was truthful. She never told me where she was going and I never thought to question her. Her business was her business.

He seemed to believe me. He relaxed and slid back into the lounger so he could put his feet up.

We both sat there for a few seconds without saying anything. Finally, he broke the ice. "You ever been in the Scouts?"

Briefly. My mother never sprang for a uniform and I routinely spent my weekly dues on five-cent packs of Batman cards. The level of commitment was low.

116

For me, it was easier to omit complicated history than hash it over.

"Nope," I lied.

He came to life and creaked the chair back into an upright position. "I think you'd like it. Roughing it. Camping out."

From outside came an unexpected swell of music followed by my mother lurching into singing, "The hills are alive with the sound of music…"

Jim's jaw dropped down in disbelief. He got up and peered out the window. "Sounds like it's comin' from next door."

She belted out a line. Jim recoiled when she nailed the top screech. "Jesus. What the hell is that?"

"That's my mother," I acknowledged.

Jim went surprisingly sheepish. "Whoa…well…"

"It's okay," I said. "Everybody knows she's crazy."

She blew a high note in fine fashion and Jim did a double-take. "Wow." He turned around and picked up an opened bottle of Seagrams 7 off an end table, then disappeared around into the kitchen to mine the fridge for 7-Up. He made a cameo in the kitchen doorway, reaching up into a cabinet. He took out one glass and dangled another.

"You want a drink?" he invited. "I'll make you a 7 and 7."

"Yeah, sure."

Jim vanished back into the kitchen.

7 and 7. Alright. I was learning a lot about cocktails in a very short amount of time. My mother was a volume drinker

so she seldom bothered taking the time to make proper cocktails. This wasn't like my mother's drinking at all. This was grown up civilized partying.

I heard Jim clunk ice cubes into glasses and splash our drinks together. He came out and handed one off to me. I sipped it. Damn. It was pretty good. Kind of sweet. I took a bigger swallow. It went down smooth.

It didn't take long for the fuzzy knit cap to settle around my head.

And that's about all I remember.

A phone rang and it woke me up. I opened my eyes. Lights were on in the room. I had to think about where I was. I looked around. Dorothy's room. On top of her bed with all my clothes on. Still drunk.

I heard Jim talking on the phone in the living room. From his responses, I knew it was my mother on the line. I staggered in and Jim passed the phone to me. The old lady was pissed.

"You were supposed to be home an hour ago! I was getting ready to call the police! How was I supposed to know where you were?"

Like she gave a shit.

I made every attempt not to give my condition away, but my mouth was having problems putting words together. "Mom, I'm fine. I just want to stay over here for a while."

"No, you're wearing your welcome out over there."

"I'm not wearing my welcome out."

"No, I want you home! Now be home in five minutes!"

She hung up in my ear.

As I put the receiver back in the cradle, I wondered how I was going to make myself appear sober. "She wants me to come home."

"Yeah, she told me," Jim said. "Well, I've got news for ya, you're not goin'."

I felt woozy, so I sat down. "But I've gotta go."

"No, you don't. You're in no condition to go home. Hey, she's so drunk, she'll be passed out in five minutes and she'll forget she ever called."

"I don't know. She's got a memory like an elephant."

My argument didn't matter, even to me.

I nodded out sitting straight up.

I woke up stretched across Dorothy's couch. It was dark. Oh, shit. I checked my surroundings. I was alone. I hopped up, rubbed my face, and smoothed out my clothes. I heard snoring. I followed the sound down the hallway to Dorothy's bedroom where I saw Jim splayed across the bed on top of the covers. He hadn't even taken his shoes off. Out like a light.

I left and went next door to my place.

My mother had locked me out. I used my key to get in.

All the curtains were drawn in the living room. My eyes had trouble adjusting from dark to darker.

I turned on a small lamp.

It was shortly after midnight. The witching hour.

No one home.

Oh, but wait.

At least this time she'd left a note.

My mother tried to kill herself several times that summer. Always by drowning in the Atlantic Ocean. But she never did it right; she went to the rocky beach up the road from us when the tide was out. To me, that made it more for show than anything else.

Elvis was still up. His dad was out for the night and my big friend volunteered to go with me to bring my mother back. I knew exactly where she'd be, out near the water's edge with her feet stuck in the muck—wailing at the moon with her nightdress half-open, her putrid breath reeking of alcohol.

There were more than a few times I wished she'd had the guts to see it through. Of course, I never considered what might happen to me as a result if she did. But that's how I felt that night.

We located her silhouette out in the mud. We each took an arm and walked her back. Got her inside. Wiped her face off with a damp facecloth. Eased her into bed. Slipped off her wet dirty shoes and covered her up.

As Elvis lined up her shoes along the wall, she slobbered, "You mush lemme sing you opera sometime!"

Elvis humored her even though she was hammered into oblivion. "Ma'am, that's the nicest offer I've had all day, but I have to decline because of my father. He doesn't allow for any of that artsy stuff."

"I should talk to him."

Elvis didn't have to respond. She fell out.

Elvis never said how fucked up this was. It went without saying. He helped without asking questions. And we never talked about it after the fact.

Elvis left and I shut the lights off on my way to bed. As I passed my mother's room, I looked in on her one more time. Still breathing.

When I went into my room, I halted at the doorway. I think I even took a step back. Every one of my 624 Beatles cards had been ripped and torn into ragged stamp-sized pieces, scattered across my bed.

It took me a while to clean it up because I kept finding orphaned fragments in unexpected nooks and crannies.

When I confronted her about it the next morning, she didn't even remember doing it.

Steve Oreno dropped the bomb on us while we were finishing our pizza.

"So we have a problem, my friends," he started out.

There were never any problems in Steve Oreno land, so we were concerned.

"No more MetBrew," he announced as he wiped off the counter with a cloth.

"Why not?" Elvis asked.

Steve's blood pressure was up—you could tell. "I had some fuckin' inspectors in here—I guess it has some microscopic amount of alcohol in it and I can't sell it without a liquor license."

Elvis leaned back in his chair. "That's fucked up."

"Tell me about it. I've got cases of it."

I sat up straight. "Give it to us."

"I can't sell it to you," Steve reasoned.

I wasn't giving up so easy. "So what are you gonna do—throw it away?"

"I have to. Of course, for about five bucks a case, you could say you found it on the dump."

I wasn't seeing through this at all. "Jesus Christ. We have to go to the dump to get it?"

Elvis and Steve eye-rolled me simultaneously.

Elvis and I guzzled a lot of MetBrew over the next few weeks. We hid cans in various meeting spots in the woods and drank them piss warm. Even unchilled, the thrill was undiminished. Getting drunk, or in our case, fantasizing we were getting drunk, brought out a testosteroned argumentative side.

One of our favorite subjects was spies. We argued the minutia. Broke each other's balls.

"James Bond—Sean Connery—could kick both Napoleon Solo's and Illya Kuryakin's asses," Elvis bragged.

I'd try not to let it get to me. "I don't know, man. Illya's the guy for me."

Elvis sniped, "Maybe if the fuckin' *Girl* from U.N.C.L.E. was helpin'."

Elvis burped a deep one, crunched his can, and tossed it into the woods. He pulled a rumpled Winston pack out of his shirt pocket, fished around in the foil, and pulled out the least bent cigarette. He stuck it in his mouth.

"I stole some smokes from my old man. You want one?"

"Nah."

He struck a match and lit up. He knew I wasn't smoking much, not since the "shoot till you win" episode where I was briefly coughing up spots of blood after smoking a hundred cigarettes without stopping in between.

Elvis took a long drag. Exhaled. Flexed. He flicked his ash with confidence. "I've said it before, I'll say it again. We need to get into something different."

"Like what?" I asked with not more than a little trepidation.

"We need to get into chicks," he pontificated. "And I'm not talkin' about Penny on *Lost in Space* either. I'm talkin' about naked chicks."

I was leery. But don't get me wrong, I was also immediately on board with the plan no matter what the plan was.

"How we gonna do that?" I asked.

Playboy

The *Playboy*s were at LaVerdiere's drug store, restricted to the top of a large wooden magazine rack. They'd nailed a slat across the Holy Grail shelf so all you could see were titles of the men's magazines. You had to be 18 to buy one. With ID.

Hence, the need to shoplift.

The first time we attempted a heist, we stood at the rack together. Elvis pulled out a *Life* and leafed through it.

Elvis coaxed me. "Go ahead. Do it."

I wasn't completely sold on the aspects of our pre-planned caper, but the forbidden fruit was hanging too low. I reached for the top shelf.

"Hey, boys," I heard the druggist say. Mr. Cadaver. That wasn't his real name, but that's what we called him.

I snapped my hand back a little too reactionary and locked eyes over my shoulder as Elvis casually turned to the voice. Elvis looked cool. I know I looked guilty as hell.

Cadaver man was probably in his 60s. He was a stern old guy who wore Coke-bottle glasses that comically magnified his eyes when he leaned in.

"This isn't a library," he lectured. "You buy something or move on."

Outside the store, Elvis made fun of me as we high-tailed it across the parking lot. "Smooth move, Exlax."

"Hey, I have to be careful," I shot back. "He almost caught me kifing a Zero bar once. And when I stole a *Famous Monsters*, he looked at me funny."

"But he never caught you, right?"

"I had a big coat on."

"Cadaver man's stupid. You coulda pulled that off if you'd been quicker."

Elvis was pissing me off. "Alright. You think it's so easy? Why don't *you* steal it?"

Elvis dropped his attack with a wry smile and defused my outburst with, "You know why you're the main thief? 'Cause you're better at it than me."

Hmm. Nice back-handed compliment.

But I had to admit, on a good day, I was one helluva thief.

We kicked back in Elvis's trailer. Elvis was fully reclined in his dad's lounger, puffing on a cigarette, plunging both of us into a stagnant haze of blue smoke.

We ate chips and I tried to get the last scraps out of the bag.

"Watch the crumbs," Elvis cautioned.

I gestured to the atomic cloud in the room. "I'd be more worried about the fuckin' smoke. My mom would kill me."

"Nah. My dad smokes. He can't smell anything anyway. By the time he comes home, it'll be cleared out."

I felt sick to my stomach. I'd been feeling that way for a week. The summer was coming to a close and anxiety gnawed a hole from the inside.

I blurted out my fear. "School starts on Monday."

Elvis exhaled. "Yeah, so what? It was getting kinda boring just walking around all the time."

"It means I get to have my ass kicked at the bus stop again."

Elvis blew more smoke out, coughed a little, and snickered to himself. "You're such a dink sometimes. Really. You need to relax."

Sure.

Easy for him to say.

When I came home at suppertime, Bill's Cadillac was in the driveway. I could hear my mother laughing through the open windows. It was the kind of drunken laughter that doesn't welcome the intrusion of a red-headed stepchild.

I went inside anyway and my presence was an instant buzz kill. They both had lipstick smeared on their faces. My mother looked more disappointed to see me than Bill was. She pushed herself up and smoothed her dress out before excusing herself in a high-heeled wobble down the hall to the bathroom.

Bill edged himself forward on his seat and waved his cheating cocktail-clutching mitt at me. "You need to lay off your mother."

I couldn't believe this shit to save my life. "Excuse me?"

"She said you hit her."

"That's a lie," I fired back. I looked Bill right in his sauced eyes. "I already explained this to you."

"Yeah, I know," he replied. "But she says you're lyin'. She's got bruises on her arms."

"Well, I don't know how she got 'em, but she didn't get them from me."

"Oh, yes, I did," she hissed as she came back in the room.

I was unable to check my anger. "Goddammit, what the fuck are you talking about now?"

Bill turned ornery. "Watch your language!"

I aimed it right back at him. I wasn't going down without a fight. Not for something I didn't do. I pointed at her. "She's making this up! I never touched her!"

She pulled up her sleeves and exposed where she'd pounded on me days earlier. She was bruised purple where her arms had struck against my defensive block. She rubbed her wounds and pleaded her case to Bill. "See? That's where he hit me!"

"No, it isn't! I held up my hands to stop you from hitting me and that's where you banged on me!"

"You're a liar!" she yelled.

"No, you're the fuckin' liar!" I bellowed back.

Bill barked, "Cut the language!"

"Cut the *lying*!" I corrected as I spun around to leave.

Cue the door slam.

Usually it's difficult to re-enter a hostile zone once you've exited with a door slamming period at the end of your sentence. Normal people are still upset upon your return and some mending of fences is required and expected.

Alcoholics are wired differently. They have blackouts where they don't remember what they've done. Nor do they care they can't recall. Each day conjures up fresh new hell.

I returned shortly after darkness fell. Bill's car was gone. There were no lights on in our trailer. I cautiously stepped inside, flipping wall switches on as I went.

When my mother crashed on the floor, for some odd reason, it was always in the same location. I followed the stench of stale vomit. It led me to her spot where I found her lying on her side, half in, half out of the doorway into our solitary claustrophobic bathroom.

But this time, she had taken it a step further.

Black blood foamed from her mouth and nose, forming a pool that highlighted her passed out profile on the torn linoleum.

I put an index finger under her nostrils. She was breathing.

I went into my room and closed the door.

I knew better than to call a doctor.

That would just piss her off.

My Bodyguard

On the first day of school, Elvis and I crossed the street from the entrance of the trailer court to the bus stop. Moosie puffed on a cigarette and whispered confidentially to Elwood and Richard who both had grown even more Neanderthal in size and posture since I'd last seen them. God, couldn't these pricks ever move away during the summer?

I'd prayed Harry Balls would be there to shit his pants as a distraction, but he'd clearly been smart enough to move during the summer recess or he'd committed suicide—either option a viable alternative to literally getting your ass kicked every day.

Elvis and I stood off by ourselves on the sidewalk. I guess it was too much to ask that Moosie and his friends would have forgotten about me over the previous three months.

Moosie was clearly freaked out by Elvis's size. Not only that, the new tubby kid was a full head taller than Richard and Elwood. But Moosie was a bold little prick.

While Elvis watched expressionless, Moosie pantomimed a fat person waddling. His minions snickered. Elvis remained stoic. Moosie didn't perceive a threat, so he tossed his cigarette into some bushes and nodded the old "watch this" to Richard and Elwood.

Moosie scooted around behind my back and kicked me solidly in the ass. I faltered into the street. I jumped back up onto the curb and faced off with that little piece of shit.

"Cut it out."

He grinned from ear to ear, exposing his over-sized front teeth. "Or what, dink?"

I moved in the opposite direction and Richard blocked me.

"Hey, fuckchops, you remember me?"

"Yeah," I acknowledged. "Dick." Okay, I couldn't resist.

"It's Richard, you little—"

Moosie cut our exchange short by shoving me back in the street.

I came back to the curb more combative. "Cut the shit, you little shrimp."

That was a mistake. Short guys take that stuff personal. Especially when you insult with intent. It just came out. I couldn't help myself.

Moosie's ears pricked up in mock I-can't-believe-you-just-said-that mode. He crowded into my personal space and cracked me across the face with an open hand. I stood solid even though I couldn't help tears welling up in my eyes.

Richard and Elwood circled closer in case their services were required.

Moosie saw the moisture in my eyes and chuckled. "You gonna cry now, trailer park boy?"

He reached back to smack me again, but before he could bring it home, Elvis lurched forward and grabbed Moosie's wrist. In one motion, he twisted Moosie's arm behind his back and forced him to the ground.

Genuinely surprised at the retaliation, Moosie got up warily and backed off a couple of steps.

Richard and Elwood had no idea how to respond, so they stood there like mannequins.

"Lay off," Elvis said. There was no need for further clarification.

Moosie was livid at the comeuppance. He rubbed his injured arm and burned a stare into me, and if looks could kill, I would've been dead ten times over.

I'd never asked Elvis to be my bodyguard.

He just did it.

On the bus, Elvis and I sat side by side on a bench seat.

Elvis stared at me in disbelief. "So why didn't you hit him back, dumb ass?"

I glanced back at Richard and Elwood, then swung back to Elvis. "Moosie comes with attachments."

Elvis wasn't buying it. "Don't let him do that to ya. They ain't gonna do shit. They're pussies. Trust me on this one thing."

For me, depending on what day it was, trust was a hard thing to come by.

On the second day of school, Moosie figured out Elvis and I were in different classes and our schedules didn't always match up.

Moosie, Richard, and Elwood cornered me in the cafeteria where I sat alone at the end of a long table minding my own business. They towered over me with menace stamped across their foreheads.

Moosie sat down across from me.

Richard reached over to a nearby trash barrel and dragged it to the edge of the table.

Moosie used his left arm to sweep my lunch tray off into the garbage.

"Lunch is over for you," he announced.

I was frozen. Fork in mid-air.

Elwood slapped the back of my head. I took it like a stump when I should've stabbed him in the heart.

Moosie stood up, bent over the table, and got nose to nose. "Listen up, free lunch boy."

Elwood cuffed the back of my head again. "You listening?"

Richard saw my fist clench around the utensil. He grabbed my fork away from me and tossed it in the trash.

Finally, the message Moosie had come to deliver. "I don't know who your fatso friend is, but he don't scare me."

"That's funny. You looked scared."

Elwood clopped me in the head again. When would I learn to pick my battles?

"You think you're clever, carrot-top?" Moosie ridiculed. "Well, just remember this. I'm going to be waiting for you. And you may think that big stupid cocksucker is going to protect you, but there'll come a day when he's not around. And then I'm gonna take care of you. I will have my way you little cunt."

Moosie eased off and led his pack away, although Elwood hung back long enough to shove me off the end of the bench onto the floor. He smirked as he swiveled away.

"You better watch yourself."

Recess always equaled cacophony. Our school handled first through eighth grade. Kids were expected to act right and police themselves accordingly in threatening situations. As long as no one screamed murderously or actually spurted blood, no adult paid notice and we were left to our own devices.

Elvis had me captive on the see-saw. He was so heavy he could hold his end down, suspending me up in the air effortlessly for long periods of time.

"Okay," I pleaded. "This is bullshit. Let me down."

Elvis cocked an eyebrow. "You want me to let down?"

"Yeah. C'mon, man. Don't do this. Don't do the thing where you jump off."

"You sure you want me to let you down?"

I saw the twinkle in his eye. "C'mon, don't—"

He didn't even let me finish the sentence before he hopped off his end and let me crash down with a wooden clunk on the hard ground.

When he was a dick, I could get away with calling him on it.

"Elvis, you asshole. I told you not to do that."

He grinned. "It's funny."

I stood up and rubbed my tailbone where my spine had been compressed. "That's just stupid shit."

Elvis countered with, "You fell for it. So who's stupid—you or me?"

Elvis veered toward the school building.

I ran to catch up with him. "See you after school at the bus stop?"

"Yup."

After school, Elvis and I waited for the bus to go home.

Behind us, Elwood and Richard held a 5th grader by his arms while Moosie fished money out of the poor sucker's pockets. Everything Moosie pulled that wasn't money was thrown to the winds. Once the shakedown was complete, Moosie slapped the kid in the face and kicked him in the nuts.

"That's what you get for being stupid," he admonished.

Moosie signaled his boys and they threw the kid to the ground in a heap.

The three hoods talked amongst themselves as they eyed us from a distance.

Moosie

He came to our haunt. Steve Oreno's turf. *Our* turf.

After the school bus dumped kids off, Elvis's dad was rarely home and my mother was already hammered if she wasn't working. We were pretty much on our own. The beauty of going to Steve's right after school was being the only patrons at that time of the day. I think our company was appreciated during the slow time before dinner.

Steve heard a quarter drop into the jukebox and poked his head out of the kitchen. "Oh, Christ, I don't even have to ask. You're gonna wear those records out."

Elvis punched in the selection numbers. Since he was buying, he got to pick, which was fine by me because he always played the music we both wanted to hear.

Steppenwolf's *Magic Carpet Ride* swelled into the room. We hooted and played drums with our hands on the table top.

Elvis's other selections played. *The Ballad of John and Yoko. Born to Be Wild.*

Steve whisked our pizza out of the kitchen onto our table. "Here you go, gentlemen. Double pepperoni with sausage. Extra sauce, extra cheese." We dug in.

I coughed up a quarter and punched in the next three: *Old Brown Shoe*, *Sookie, Sookie* and *The Ballad of John and Yoko* again.

Steve shook his head in mock disgust as he bagged up trash.

No doubt about it. This was our home.

The screen door creaked open and Moosie appeared in the threshold. He cased the joint for a moment or two before crossing over into our territory.

Elvis and I went formal. Guarded.

Steve addressed his new customer. "Hey, how ya doin'? What can I get ya?"

Moosie approached and quickly scanned the hand-painted menu posted on the wall behind the counter.

"I'll take a medium pepperoni."

Steve smiled broadly. "Great. Be about 10 minutes. There's drinks in the case over there while you're waiting."

"Thanks," Moosie said.

Steve went in the back.

Moosie moseyed over to the jukebox right as *The Ballad of John and Yoko* started. In a much too loud voice, he exclaimed, "God, who played this piece of shit song?"

We ignored him.

"It's so old-fashioned," he whined.

He gripped his hands on the Seeburg's sides and rocked the jukebox back and forth. The record skipped all the way to the end and the music came to an abrupt halt.

The instant silence was punctuated by the sound of Steve sliding Moosie's pizza into the oven.

I jumped up. "Hey!"

Steve poked his head out of the kitchen. "What's going on, gentlemen?"

"Nothin'," Moosie lied. "I tripped over something on your floor."

"That's a lie," I finked.

Steve came into the room and stink-eyed us like we were in a line-up. "What happened?"

I pointed at Moosie. "He pushed the jukebox to make it skip."

Steve put his hands on his hips and faced off with Moosie. "Is that true?"

"Hell, no," Moosie fumed.

Steve was exasperated. "Guys—"

"Hey, screw this," Moosie said as he turned and strode out the door.

Steve called after him. "Hey, you owe me four bucks!"

Steve ran to the door, but Moosie was gone. "That little—"

"Moosie," I offered.

"Yeah, I know his first name—what's his last name?" Steve asked.

Elvis and I both shrugged—neither one of us knew.

"You know him?" I asked.

"Yeah. His dad owns a garage up the road. I'll go talk to that little shit's parents. He better never come in here again!"

Steve got a grip on himself. "Sorry, guys. I don't mean to take it out on you, but that really pissed me off."

Believe me, we understood. Steve's business was struggling. Anyone who screwed him out of money was an asshole in our book. And Moosie was already an asshole in our book, so he was two volumes of asshole.

When Moosie's pizza was done, Steve gave it to us rather than toss it. Elvis tried to give Steve the four dollars, but Steve wouldn't take it. So Elvis left it as a tip.

Moosie never came back.

His lingering legacy at Steve Oreno's was the record he messed up. It skipped permanently in one place right at the end of the bridge where John nails the word "Think!"

Blasphemy. I wanted Moosie to rot in hell.

We played it anyway.

The Catcher in the Rye

Brian Jones was nondescript, even for an English teacher. Sandy hair and wire-framed glasses. Pudgy in the face and around his waistline. Probably in his early 30s. He was a weird amalgam of hippie and professor. But in my particular case, the bottom line with Mr. Jones was that he always treated me with kindness.

I enjoyed his classes, unlike the drudgery of all the others I sat through. He was hip. Cool. Slightly dangerous. He often strayed from the core values of education and sought to teach us things that mattered. He encouraged us to be rebellious as well. Especially in our creative writing assignments for the class. I was granted the freedom to write unbridled.

If Mr. Jones needed to cement his relationship with his students, he did it in one fell swoop the day he abandoned his lesson plan and brought in a copy of *Sergeant Pepper's Lonely Hearts Club Band*. Number one, it was unusual for a teacher to not follow the rules. Number two, if a teacher did cartwheel off into left field, they did something more along the lines of throwing a blackboard eraser past your head to get your attention at the back of the room. They never went nuts and played cuts from a Beatles' album.

It was understood without saying that Mr. Jones took a risk being unconventional. We had great respect for his courage. If they'd had Salem teacher trials, Brian would have been the first one they burned at the stake.

He played two selections for us that day. The songs themselves played out in 6 or 7 minutes, but he wanted to actually *discuss* the merits of the music with particular emphasis on interpretations of the lyrics. We didn't have a clue how to act.

First, he played *Lucy in the Sky with Diamonds*. You could have heard a pin drop in the room. There was absolute reverence for this experiment we were being asked to take part in. We discussed the imagery and beauty of the words.

The second track he queued up was *She's Leaving Home* and he was so emotionally struck by the import of the lyrics, he read them aloud to us before playing the song. It's a story about a young girl who runs away from home and her parents don't understand. They feel like they gave her everything money could buy. When he got to the point where he recited, "Daddy, our baby's gone," I thought he might cry. His voice caught right in the middle of the line. He managed to collect himself and summarized with, "Let's just play it. It's a piece of art."

I'd never seen a man become emotional about art before. I was in awe of this gentle man who didn't seem ashamed when his emotions gave him away. When he lifted the needle at the end of the track, the room was silent.

"Beautiful. Just beautiful," he said softly as he put the album back in its paper sleeve.

Mr. Jones could care less if you did your homework. He wanted you to get smart by any means necessary. He treated us as young adults and we responded accordingly.

I wrote reams of short stories in English class. Mr. Jones often read what his students wrote out loud without identifying the author. I was thrilled because my stuff got read more than anyone else's. Nobody knew my secret. I loved watching the facial reactions of my classmates as they listened to my words.

One afternoon, after the bell rang signaling recess, Mr. Jones held me back as I attempted to exit with the rush. I stood off to the side watching my classmates crush each other to get out the door. He sat casually on the edge of his desk and waited for us to be alone.

Once they'd all filed out, Mr. Jones swiveled to face me. "All right." He had a twinkle in his tone that matched the one in his eye. "If anyone asks, we never had this conversation."

Already I was intrigued. Being in a conspiracy with an adult was always heady stuff. And I had no reason to fear this guy. I didn't say anything. I just listened.

"I've enjoyed your writing immensely."

I puffed up a little and nodded my thanks.

He picked up on my puff-up and sprinkled a bit of caution around the room. "By the same token, some might toy with the idea of having you committed for some of the things you write down on paper."

My face must have fallen because he quickly assuaged my wound with a coy smile that told me he was joking. Sort of.

"There's a book I think you might enjoy reading."

Oh, God. An outside assignment. This was the last thing I wanted on my plate. He must have seen my thoughts written across my forehead because he segued right away to the teaser he thought might bring the bait within reach.

"I can't actually give you the book or teach it in class because it's not allowed."

My ears perked like an elf.

"It's called *The Catcher in the Rye*," he continued. "It's written by an author named J. D. Salinger."

I'd never heard of it. He could tell by my blank expression.

"It's in every public library. I think you should check it out. It might appeal to you."

Consider it done.

The next day was Saturday. I pedaled a few miles to the Rockland library. The building was centered in the middle of a thick well-manicured lawn. I got there when the doors opened at 9 AM. I went through the card catalog and wrote down the information I needed.

As I padded past reading tables and walls of meticulously filed books in cavernous rooms with high ceilings, I felt a feeling of well-being wash over me. There was calm and insulation when I was surrounded by books. Always.

I didn't find my book. J. D. Salinger's masterpiece was checked out.

Since I was in the library anyway, I opted to plunk down in a plush leather arm chair by a French window in a secluded corner. I didn't read a book. I didn't want to. I didn't want to do anything but sit there and watch fall leaves blow along the sidewalks.

At one point, a gentle hunched over librarian with thin white hair stopped in front of me and asked if she could help me find something. Nope. I was happy with the serenity.

I sat there until lunchtime watching rusted leaves drift down to the ground.

I thought about how restful it was to my eyes.

The following Monday at school, I got my study hall teacher to write me a library pass at the beginning of 3rd period. Originally, I was going to spend some time with our school library's copy of *The American Slang Dictionary*, but on a hunch, I looked up Salinger's book in the card drawers.

And there it was. Right under my nose the whole time. What good fortune was this?

I was getting pretty savvy about the layout of the library and I latched onto that book in 2 minutes with no adult supervision. A solid red cover with white letters. It was an older edition, well-read. I liked the smell of the pages.

After locating the most secluded empty reading table, I sat down to begin my journey through Holden Caulfield's world of alienated observation. *The Catcher in the Rye* was the first book I'd read that explored teen angst at a deeply emotional level. I was hooked from page one. Reading Holden's story made me feel normal and that was a most unusual feeling indeed.

I didn't dare check it out. I wasn't sure they'd let me. Plus if my mother found it, she might go off the rails and destroy it in a rage. Then I'd have to cough up money to replace a library book.

No problem. I could knock out the read in study halls without ever taking the book out.

And that's exactly what I did for the next two weeks.

Knowledge is power and I was absorbing as fast as cheap toilet paper. I didn't tell Elvis about the book until we were riding home on the bus at the end of the first week. He wanted to read it too, but I convinced him not to draw any attention to the situation because there was only one copy. We couldn't read it together in a public setting without looking like a pair of homos.

Elvis came up with an alternative plan. We'd trade off and whichever one of us wasn't reading about Holden Caulfield could spend their time scoping the African natives in back issues of National Geographic. Although that was a mixed bag. You'd stumble upon young pert breasts that were attractive, but they were usually surrounded by worn out toothless hags with pancake tits.

One had a way of canceling the other out.

Elvis didn't know the library terrain like I did. So after he failed to find the book on his own, I went with him during a recess to show him where the novel was. As luck would have it, right when I pulled the book off the shelf from between its mates, the oldest and crabbiest of all the school librarians, Miss Burke, rounded the corner and caught us red-handed.

Miss Burke was tight-assed and did not suffer fools lightly. Not a hair out of place. Tobacco on her breath. She dressed us up and down like we'd put a turd in the punchbowl. We froze. There was no case to make. We were at her mercy.

She looked icily over her glasses and assessed the situation.

"That's an interesting book you have in your hands," she said sternly.

"Yes, ma'am," I quivered in reply.

"There are a lot of adult themes in that novel."

"Yes, ma'am." Man, I was a wordsmith.

"There are many who would not approve of you reading it at your age."

"Yes, ma'am." Jesus, could I sound any more stupid?

She studied us for what seemed like minutes. "Very well, then. Keep it quiet." She walked away without ceremony.

Elvis and I stared at each other in amazement.

It was obvious there were all kinds of people who knew the power of that book.

In English class, Mr. Jones had just finished reading aloud to us when the recess bell rang. The stampede ensued, and Mr. Jones motioned for me to remain behind.

When we were alone, he smiled like the Cheshire cat. "A little birdie told me you've been making a lot of trips to the school library lately."

"Yeah, I read that book you told me." Nice grammar in front of the English teacher.

"What'd you think?"

I didn't have to say a word. He could tell by the expression on my face the story had spoken to my soul.

"I'm glad you liked it," he said as he waved me out of the room. "Go enjoy your recess."

As I went to leave, he held up an index finger. "Oh, and one other thing."

"What?"

"I never talked to you, okay?"

"Talked to me about what?"

He smiled at me and I sealed the deal with a smile back.

And that was it with Mr. Brian Jones. He never again suggested reading material to me. I think in his teacher mind it was mission accomplished. He knew that singular experience would lead me down reading paths for the rest of my life.

He'd done what teachers are supposed to do.

He'd given me a great gift.

Abbey Road

I continued to baby-sit for Dorothy. Elvis often hung out with me. We were still never sure where Dorothy was going and we never asked.

One Saturday afternoon in early October, she breezed in carrying a flat bag under her arm.

"Hey, guys. Look what I got."

She reached into the bag and pulled out a fresh copy of *Abbey Road.*

I inched closer. "Is that The Beatles?"

"Just came out and I was there and said, 'What the hell.'"

She expertly slit the shrink wrap with a pink polished fingernail and slid the fresh vinyl out onto a waiting palm as if it possessed some mystical secret.

Elvis sat up a bit. "Shit, I didn't even know they had something new coming out."

We usually had no way of knowing when new releases would drop from the sky. We'd just *hear* a new song somewhere. Or walk by a record store and see some cardboard prop advertising a new album or single. And a new Beatles release was something on another level all by itself. They *never* disappointed.

Dorothy placed the album onto her turntable and lowered the tone arm.

We sat glued around her stereo cabinet like some old family in the 1920s listening to the radio. It was magical. From start to finish. Flawless. But coming from The Beatles, we had come to expect nothing less.

A few songs in, Elvis lit three cigarettes simultaneously. He handed one to Dorothy, one to me, and kept one for himself.

We listened to the whole thing—both sides—four times in a row.

And then I had to go home.

Home to what.

My mother was well into the 16-ouncers again.

I begged to go back and spend the night at Dorothy's. "She asked me if I could spend the night to watch her kid and it's not a school night—"

My mother wasn't sold. "I don't know. What if something happens?"

"Darrell'll be there." I knew she sort of liked him, but probably only because she didn't know him well enough. I made sure to add, "And we're right next door."

Of course, this was all a ruse. Dorothy was going to be home, but we were going to drink and I didn't want to have to return home and get found out.

I think my mother looked at it as another opportunity to get plastered in her living room without any interference from a family member. We enabled each other.

She waved her half-assed hand of approval.

Elvis and I sat cross-legged like disciples in front of Dorothy's coffee table, staring at tumblers she'd filled with ice cubes.

She cracked a quart-sized thick green glass bottle of Coke and reached into her purse. She brought out a small slender brown-paper bag with a pint of Bacardi white rum inside. When she pulled the bottle out of its sheath, we both ogled it like it was a solid bar of gold from Fort Knox.

"You can't tell anybody," Dorothy warned as she expertly mixed the drinks.

It was my first rum and Coke. Served by the barmaid of my dreams. We toasted. Sipped our drinks. It was nectar from the Gods.

And man, did I get fucked up in a hurry.

We laughed hysterically.

I got blind drunk. Blacked out. The only part I remember is waking up later slobbering and breathing heavily over

Dorothy as she cooked up Kraft Macaroni and Cheese. She served it on paper plates and we stood up to eat.

I was ravenous and loud. "*Goddammit!* This is fucking *great!*"

Elvis nodded in agreement. "Um-*hmm*."

Dorothy thought our allegiance was funny. "It's just out of a box, silly."

"No! This is *great!*" I raved. "Goddam, you can *cook!*"

I weaved in place and set my half-eaten plate down on the counter.

Dorothy sensed I was in trouble. "You alright, Tim?"

The liquor had unpleasant effects on a colossal level. "Yeah, I'm fine," I lied.

Elvis was in Dorothy's corner. "You don't *look* fine."

Dorothy came closer. "No, really, sweetie, are you okay?"

I thought I might be sick, so I instinctively stumbled toward a door in her kitchen that led to the outside. "I need some fresh air," I heard myself say.

Dorothy tried to stop me. "Tim, there's no steps. Tim!"

Too late. I'd popped the door and stepped outside, with that last step being a face first onto the grass and weeds four feet below. I was so disoriented, I'd forgotten her kitchen door opened into thin air.

I rolled over in the dirt and looked up at Elvis peering down at me. "Oh, shit!" he whispered.

Dorothy appeared in the open doorway beside him. They pulled the door closed. For a minute, I thought they'd left me and gone back to partying. I needed to purge. I rolled over on my stomach and puked. Everything came up all at once. It was a relief. Perfunctory.

I rolled back over and sensed Elvis and Dorothy standing over me. They helped me get to my feet. I was feeling no pain. Trashed. Giggling.

"You okay, honey?" Dorothy asked, followed by "Jesus" under her breath.

"Naw, I'm fine," I laughed.

Dorothy draped one of my arms around her neck as Darrell took the opposite side. "C'mon, Darrell. Let's get him inside."

I had to put one foot on the floor to stop the spins while I was lying on her couch. Although I had great affection for little baby Gene, it was all I could do to not push him away when he came over and patted me on the leg.

Elvis seemed to have no problem with his intake. He hovered over me and assessed my condition. "He'll be alright."

Hey, fucker, how would you know?

Dorothy came over and put a cold wet washcloth on my forehead. I appreciated being nursed.

"Oh, Tim," she said soft as velvet. "Are you okay?"

In fact, I was far from okay. I bolted upright. "Okay, I can't lie down right now," I announced. Nobody argued the point.

Dorothy backed up. "You gonna be sick again?"

I gurgled a little. I sounded like my mother and that struck me as funny for a brief moment, but that was interrupted by something vile creeping up the back of my throat.

Dorothy got all business. "No, really, Tim. If you're going to throw up, let's get to the bathroom or outside."

"No, I'm fine," I reassured her as I turned greener in front of their eyes.

Elvis burst out laughing. "No, you're definitely *not* fine!"

There was a knock at the door.

Dorothy smiled knowingly. "It's okay. It's just my boyfriend."

I was reeling. Boyfriend? Oh, yeah, she'd mentioned a boyfriend.

Elvis stiffened.

Dorothy half-skipped to the door and opened it. In walked Peter. I had to admit, he was beautiful. Dashing. Muscular. Blond and blue-eyed.

He kissed Dorothy hello with authority and it was a dagger through my heart.

"Hey, Dottie," he smarmed as he grabbed her ass from behind.

Already I didn't like him. I would never embarrass someone in public like that. Whether I liked them or not.

He surveyed the company in the room and laughed. "What's goin' on?"

Dorothy went straight to introductions. "Peter, this is Darrell."

Elvis nodded from the chair ever so slightly.

I slid off the edge of the couch into a lump of debris on the floor.

Dorothy gestured to me. "And that's Tim."

Peter flashed a million-dollar smile that reminded me of Bill's phony shit. "Hi, guys. Nice to meet you."

He bent down and helped me back up onto the couch. He was strong as an ox. Lifted me with one arm. "You okay, Tim?" He almost sounded like he cared.

"Yeah, I'm fine," I fibbed.

Dorothy pointed at Elvis. "Darrell, can you watch Gene?"

Elvis nodded in the affirmative.

Then she pointed at me. "And take care of him."

Elvis raised his rum and Coke from his kingly position nestled in the overstuffed recliner. "Sure. No problem."

Dorothy kissed Peter as she put an arm around his waist. "Hi, Pete. Thanks for coming over."

Through my fog of inebriation, I watched her lead Peter down the hallway to her bedroom. They went in and closed the door behind them.

I wanted to run down the hall, break in, and tear them apart.

She was mine.

Elvis adjusted the blanket on Gene who was sequestered on one end of the couch. I sat on the other end.

Once Elvis was sure Gene was sound asleep, he shifted over to the recliner and contentedly piled himself back into comfort.

I thought I might heave again at any moment.

Even though I felt like I wasn't worthy of Dorothy's affections, I still wanted them. I nodded toward Dorothy's bedroom. "What's goin' on in there?"

"You don't wanna know," Elvis warned as he pulled a blanket up over his head.

No, I really didn't want to know. But I was jealous as hell and the intensity hit me like a tidal wave.

There was a loud squeak from down the hall.

"They're doin' it." I had a stranglehold on the obvious.

Elvis peeked over his blanket and yawned. "Hey, they could be playing checkers or something," he quipped as he lit a cigarette.

His humor wasn't appreciated and the smell of his smoke was making me feel more ill than I already felt.

Another squeak.

I felt myself going into tunnel-vision. I was forced to concede. "No, they're definitely doing it."

Elvis blew out a smoke ring. "Shut up. What do you care?"

"But I do," I admitted, and the second it slipped out, I wished I could've taken it back.

Elvis offered his professional opinion. "Dude, you're not even in his league. You've never even *done* it and now you wanna take her on?"

"Well, what about you?" I sharked back. "You've never done it either."

Elvis smiled slyly. "Yeah, I have."

This was news to me. "With who?"

Elvis arched his eyebrows. "Your mom."

And without thinking it through, I did something I'd never done. I reached over and punched him on the arm. I hit him hard—well, hard for me—but he was so thick, it barely registered.

Elvis blew it off. "God, you're such a homo. No wonder you can't kick Moosie's ass."

That was the wrong button to push. I went from zero to eleven in a heartbeat. My rage made my head swell. I jumped up and punched Elvis in the arm even harder. With meanness attached.

My intent wasn't lost on Elvis. He sat up straight. He'd had enough. "Hey, you little peckerhead!"

I was so blind with emotion, I pulled back to slug him again. His reflexes were surprisingly fast. He intercepted my fist as I brought it in for another landing. He twisted up out of his chair, countered my force, and flipped me around so I ended up chest down on the couch with my face mashed into a cushion. He slid in on top of me and plopped his double-wide ass down on top of my head. This was not entirely cool because he was pretty fucking heavy. I thought my skull might explode under the pressure and Elvis didn't seem to care at all.

"Get off me, you big sonofabitch!" I yelled, although the end product was all muffle.

"Wait just a minute," Elvis announced. "I feel something coming on."

And then Elvis did something he'd never done. He positioned his butt crack so it was solid against my face with no breathing room.

I struggled against him fruitlessly. "Cut it out, you fat—"

Elvis let off a big one. Major ass trumpet.

I was furious, but unable to escape.

"Stop! You're killing me!"

Elvis sprung up off my head to a standing position and dragged on his cigarette, just daring me to try something else. "There. Now stop the bullshit."

I was pissed. I sat up. Gene fussed. We'd woken him.

Without catching Elvis's gaze, I let my thoughts be known. "You suck."

I felt a mist forming in my eyes. I couldn't stop it. Elvis had no pity. He referenced Gene fussing. "Now look what you did." He turned back to me. "You gonna cry now?"

Truth be known, I wanted to.

Dorothy tip-toed in wrapped in a bathrobe, pushing her mussed up hair out of her face. "Hey, what's going on out here?" she asked with wide-eyed concern.

Elvis puffed out a smoke ring. "Oh, nothing. Just wrestling."

Dorothy bent down to coo at Gene and he fell back asleep instantly. She looked up at both of us and whispered, "C'mon, guys. Act right or go home."

That was all I needed. To be spoken to like a child. I went into a serious pout. I didn't say anything, just picked up my coat and before I walked out the door, I heard Dorothy ask "What's the matter with him?" like I wasn't in the room.

"Beats me," deadpanned my best friend.

I went out the door. As I went to close it, I wanted to slam it as hard as I could.

But I didn't.

Sorry

Elvis farted on my drunk face on a Friday night. We needed a cooling off period. We didn't see each other all day Saturday and that was fine by me. I went to the Rockland library in the morning and spent the afternoon attempting to collect money from customers on my paper route.

I spent hours riding around on my rickety Wonder Bike, knocking on people's doors. Most folks were decent, but it only takes a couple of bad clowns to fuck up the circus. I never understood the unwillingness to part with a damned dollar. I mean, they were stiffin' the goddam *paperboy*, for Chrissakes. Didn't they feel the least little bit guilty about that? Apparently, they did not. It never failed that I had people who would close their curtains when they saw me coming.

Hey, just don't order the paper.

I mean, how hard is this?

Elvis and I made up on Sunday afternoon. There wasn't much talking. You didn't apologize to friends, you just waited for storms to pass.

It was a cool, fall day.

There was an emotional distance between us. A wall.

We walked side by side. Slowly.

Not looking at each other.

The next morning at the bus stop, Moosie tortured a grade-school girl with pigtails. He started by throwing her books on the ground. Elwood and Richard hooted maniacally.

Elvis and I stood off to the side doing our best to ignore the situation.

Moosie yanked hard on her pigtails. She started to cry and that was it. Elvis had had enough.

He moved on Moosie with purpose and Moosie immediately let the girl go.

Richard and Elwood hung back.

Elvis towered over Moosie. "Hey, shit-for-brains. Pick up her stuff."

Moosie didn't do it.

Elvis faked a punch and Moosie flinched. That was license if your target flinched. Elvis grabbed Moosie and punched him solidly on the upper arm. The slapping thud it made told you it got deep into the muscle tissue. Elvis was getting into it. I was seeing a side of him I'd never seen before—a dangerous side.

"Two for flinching," Elvis decreed.

Moosie tried to pull away, but Elvis had a lock on him. Elvis ham-hocked Moosie even harder and tossed him aside.

Moosie wheeled around to his support act. "Back me up!"

Richard didn't attempt to move. Elwood was stupid enough to step up to the plate. Elvis didn't hesitate—he charged Elwood and shoved him with such force, Elwood fell back into Richard causing them both to crumble to the sidewalk.

Elvis challenged Richard and Elwood to get up. They remained in submission.

Elvis wasn't done. He grabbed Moosie by the neck of his shirt, lifted him up on his tip-toes, and threw him down toward the little girl's books on the ground.

"Now. Pick up her stuff."

Moosie was shaking mad, but he slowly obeyed. He trained his dark eyes on Elvis the whole time. Elvis wasn't the least bit intimidated.

Moosie begrudgingly handed the girl her books.

"Tell her you're sorry," Elvis insisted.

Moosie's jaw dropped. What? He puffed up. "Fuck you."

Without hesitation, a big meaty Elvis bear claw jutted out and seized hold of Moosie's face, squeezing his cheeks together. Moosie turned beet red. He was scared.

Elvis drew close. "What are you—deaf?"

Richard and Elwood started to rise. Elvis twisted toward them. "Nobody told you to get up."

They got back down.

Elvis forced Moosie toward the girl with the pigtails. "Say you're sorry."

Moosie hesitated. Elvis pushed him again.

"Say it."

Moosie looked at her, then at Elvis, then back at her. Lowering his gaze, he muttered, "Sorry."

Elvis wasn't satisfied. Not by a long shot. "Like you mean it, shrimp."

Moosie shot Elvis a "you've gotta be kidding" look.

Elvis faked another swing Moosie's way. Moosie jumped back and let out a slightly more authentic apology. "Sorry!"

Elvis put a hand on Moosie's shoulder like they were buddies. "See? That was easy." Elvis grinned and ruffled Moosie's hair. Moosie wanted to kill, but wisely held his tongue.

Elvis turned to Richard and Elwood. "Okay. You can get back up now."

They did. With great caution.

The bus rumbled up and heaved to a stop. Elvis smiled at the little girl and waved her on first.

Moosie was crazy angry.

Elvis couldn't resist. "Hey, Moosie. What'd you do? Comb your hair with a rock this morning?"

Elvis didn't bother checking back over his shoulder, but I did. Moosie shot daggers at us.

He narrowed his eyes at Elvis and mouthed the words "I'll get you."

Bullies take advantage of opportunities. Moosie nibbled at me over the coming weeks when Elvis wasn't around, but he kept his distance for the most part.

For the most part.

I was getting books out of my locker in the hallway. Moosie snuck up outside my peripheral vision and banged me against the wall of lockers. He didn't say anything—just bashed into me. Being a dick.

In my next class, I stared out the window. Daydreaming. I wished I was bigger. Stronger.

More of a man.

That afternoon at Steve Oreno's, Elvis made all the selections on the Seeburg. For the first time since we'd been going there, he didn't play *The Ballad of John and Yoko*. Steve even asked him about it. Nope. Not today.

Elvis was playing other stuff. He was hot on the newest Beatles single. He played it over and over. Both sides—*Something* and *Come Together*. His quarters, his picks.

I guess we were growing apart.

But at least we were still friends.

And you couldn't help but love The Beatles no matter what they were playing.

Thanksgiving

I was babysitting a lot for Gene. Mostly during the evenings, sometimes during the daytime if it was the weekend.

We saw less and less of Dorothy.

I was dying inside every moment of the day.

I put Gene down for the night in his crib around the corner in the first bedroom and locked the front door.

Dozed off on the couch.

In the back of my head, I heard a key turning in the lock.

As I opened my eyes in the dimly lit room, I felt a presence. I bolted upright and there was Jim sitting across from me, grinning his toothy grin.

"What's up?" he asked nonchalantly.

"Guess I must have fallen asleep," I confessed.

"Where's Dottie?" His smile hardened almost imperceptibly when he said her name.

"I don't know."

He leaned forward. "What do you mean, you don't know? She must tell you where she's going. Leave a phone number. Something."

I shook my head no.

He dropped his grin and angled even closer. "Is there something going on between you and my wife?"

I gulped. "What?"

"Does she try to get with you?"

"No." I quivered inside.

An odd creepy grimace spread across his face. "You sure?"

I nodded yes without making eye contact.

He got to his feet and towered over me. "I wanna believe you."

Without looking up, I said, "I have no reason to lie to you."

Jim knelt down so we were eye to eye. "Okay, son. I believe you. You seem like a good kid."

He reached around, pinched my side, and laughed when I shied away. "You thought anymore about joining up with the Scouts?"

To me, the conversation had started out on the wrong foot and gotten stranger as we went along. I shook my head no.

He stared at me for what seemed like an eternity, then patted me on the knee and stood up. As he walked to the door, he said over his shoulder, "When you see Dottie, tell her I'm looking for her."

He gave me a little salute and was gone.

It unnerved me.

I heard Gene fuss.

Dorothy came in late. She barely made a sound.

I was on edge. Wide-awake.

She was tipsy. Unsettled. Too quiet. Ghostly even. She slipped out of her shoes and tip-toed to the couch to kneel down in front of her beloved son.

I put a "Don't wake him up" finger to my lips. Like all of a sudden, I knew more about parenting than she did.

She nuzzled Gene's sleeping face and smelled the side of his head. I got a better look at her when her face came into the half-light. She'd been crying.

"Hey, little guy," she whispered in his ear. She picked him up gently. "Let's get you to bed."

Gene stirred slightly in her arms.

"No, it's okay," she cooed as she disappeared with Gene around the corner.

I sat like a lump on the couch.

She came back in noiselessly and stood above me. "Why wasn't he in bed?"

"He was, but he woke up and seemed to do better out here."

Dorothy grabbed her purse and fished around, coming up empty-handed. "I don't have any money. Can I pay you next time?"

"Okay." I didn't want her money. I just wanted her to love me. "Somebody was here. Your husband came by to see you. He wants you to get in touch with him."

She tensed when I mentioned him. "What'd he want?"

"He didn't say."

"Okay, well…" she shrugged. She motioned toward the door. "You need to go home now."

I stood up and looked at her. I wished she'd confide in me. I wished she'd see how good I was for her. I wished she'd let me comfort her.

"Go. Please," she choked out.

So I left.

When I went back to my trailer, my mother was snoring in front of the TV with the sound jacked up. I lowered the volume. She stirred, but didn't wake.

I fell onto my bed, buried my face in my pillow and punched the side of it. I flipped over onto my back and stared at the ceiling.

I was painfully aware I was only 14. Didn't Dorothy understand that age didn't matter? Why couldn't she understand I'd still be there for her?

Why couldn't she wait?

Thanksgiving the year before had been pathetic. My mother cobbled together a bag of mixed nuts and a whole par-boiled chicken-in-a-can. Even after you cooked it, the slimy mess still had the embedded rings identifiable around the body. The skin wasn't crisp. It was like eating, well, skin. It was nasty shit.

On our first Thanksgiving in Glen Cove, my mother was obliterated by 10 AM. It looked like even a chicken-in-a-can was out of the realm of possibility.

For some reason, Elvis's dad wasn't home.

We went over and knocked on Dorothy's door, but she was gone.

So we had Thanksgiving at Steve's. We were surprised he was open, but he thought he might get some business, and news to us, he did. Without saying anything, I think Steve thought it was fucked up we didn't have anywhere else to go.

The pizza was on the house, but we compensated with all the quarters we made the Seeburg eat.

Steve enjoyed our company and even sat down with us to eat.

I don't think he had anybody either.

Later in the afternoon, we walked off the pizza by heading down to the drugstore.

We scanned the titles on the magazine racks. *Famous Monsters of Filmland* came out every 2 months and it wasn't due for weeks. In this moment, it didn't matter. A line had been drawn in the sand. We had our sights on a different prize.

Elvis scoped the store and we both locked in on the *Playboy* logo behind the top slat. Elvis caught Cadaver man watching us.

Elvis whispered, "We need a diversion."

I looked back at crazy guy. He was filling a prescription for the only other customer in the store. He kept glancing over at us.

Elvis drew me back in. "You need to keep him busy while I take care of this."

"How do I do that?"

"Go up and tell him you've got crabs. See what he says."

Crabs? What the fuck was he talking about? "And then what?"

"While he's talking to you, I'll grab the magazine."

"What are crabs?" I wanted to know.

Elvis gave me a "I'll explain later" look. "It's seafood, now just go up there."

I stalled. "Why don't you tell him *you* have crabs?"

"No, it has to be you. I'm taller so he won't see me kifing."

"But why does it have to be me? I thought I was the shoplifting expert."

"Yeah, well, change of plans. He'll believe you. Just act stupid. Keep that same look you have on your face right now."

"Is he gonna ask to see them? The crabs, I mean."

"I doubt it."

I still wasn't sold. I knew this was fucked up, I just didn't know why.

"Go," he ordered.

I approached the pharmacy section. Cadaver man tracked me with his magnified eyes. He'd rung up the prescription he'd filled and his customer walked out as I made my way up the aisle.

I was sweating bullets.

Cadaver man bent slightly forward over the glass counter. "May I help you?"

I had no idea what I was doing. "Yeah, uh—I've got some crabs."

Cadaver man's mouth fell open. A young female assistant nearby stifled a laugh.

Behind me, Elvis eased the *Playboy* out of the rack, shifted it under his coat, and walked straight out the door.

Cadaver man was uncharacteristically sympathetic. Subdued even. "So, umm—I have a cream ointment," he offered nervously. "Or a lathering—"

The assistant couldn't control herself and covered her face. That's when I made for a hasty exit. Cadaver man came around from behind the counter and sprinted after me.

"No, wait, I can help you!"

I ran out of the store and caught up with Elvis at the end of the parking lot where it leveled off into a wooded area. I huffed and puffed as I passed him. "C'mon! Let's go!"

I left Elvis in the dust. He tried running a few steps. It didn't matter because no one had followed us. We'd made a clean getaway.

After pushing our way through a block of woods, we emptied out into the trailer park. We were beat. Couldn't run anymore. Gasping. Heaving. Elvis pointed at me and laughed so hard, I thought he was going to blow a gasket.

"Oh, man! I cannot believe you did that!" he coughed out.

"Alright," I steamed. "What the fuck are crabs?"

"Never mind. It doesn't matter. God, that was funny."

"Elvis, what are they?" I pleaded.

He got a momentary grip, then sprayed out snot droplets. "I told you…"

I had to laugh a little myself. "Fuck you, man."

He lost it again. "Seafood!"

Back at Elvis's trailer, we sprawled out on the floor and pulled open the centerfold. Again. We stared in stony silence. Words were not necessary in this bonding experience.

Elvis snorted and rolled over on one side. "Crabs. Jesus, that was funny."

"Well, now that I know what they are, I need you to shut up about it. You realize I can never go in that store again."

I pointed to the centerfold. "Finished?"

"Yeah." Elvis convulsed again thinking about me and the crabs. "Oh, man."

I carefully put the centerfold back into the magazine and turned the page. "Hey, let's read the jokes again."

Elvis got control of himself and rolled over so we could read together.

That night, I locked myself in our trailer's one bathroom with the newly acquired *Playboy,* on loan to me for the night. The bathroom was the only place where my mother wouldn't barge in.

She rapped on the door. "What are you doing in there?"

"Nothing!" I yelled back, hoping that would quash her intrusion.

No such luck.

"You're taking too long!"

"Gimme a minute!"

"I need to get in there!"

Fuck.

Elvis and I spent hours in his trailer reading and re-reading every word in that stolen *Playboy.* Not to mention the time we spent drinking in the pictures, asking permission before carefully turning pages.

They didn't teach sex education in schools. Or anywhere else, for that matter. And you sure couldn't depend on your parents for anything reliable. Elvis and his dad hadn't had "the talk" yet. My mother was worthless. Trust me, *Playboy* was a godsend.

We had definitely come into possession of the Holy Grail, but some things were still unclear about the bottom half of the female anatomy. My only previous exposure had been a pile of crudely published black and white nudist colony magazines where all the women's privates were air-brushed out to make them look like Barbie dolls. And even though the photographs in *Playboy* were gorgeous, they still weren't showing you a whole lot down there.

So we guessed about shit.

Elvis laid it out. "My dad says it's the second hole down from the back of the neck."

"Well, how many holes do they have?" I wanted to know.

Elvis shrugged. He didn't know.

I was definitely stimulated by looking at the nude pictorials, but I was totally confused as to what you did with girls. So as far as we were concerned, this Hugh Hefner guy was a fuckin' genius.

Between studying his magazine's guarded pubic regions and armed with the "two holes down from the back of the neck" rule, I was almost able to put something together on how this sex thing was done.

My First Kiss

Gene was already down.

Elvis and I smoked cigarettes on opposite ends of Dorothy's couch while she bent over the stereo and put on Neil Diamond's *Sweet Caroline*. The women in *Playboy* were beyond beautiful, but I thought Dorothy ranked above them all.

As Neil came in low and manly on the vocal, Dorothy sipped on a cocktail and undulated slowly in front of us, lost in her thoughts. Neil Diamond was a tipping point for her.

She usually was happily into it, but sometimes she got sad for no reason.

Dorothy ended up passed out in a chair.

When it didn't look like she was going to revive for a while, Elvis pushed up off the couch. "I'll see ya tomorrow. I'm gonna go sleep on my own bed."

He left without making a sound.

I found a blanket and put it around Dorothy. She opened her eyes.

"Are you okay?" I asked.

"I don't feel so good."

She threw up. A lot. It wasn't like how my mother threw up. It was controlled throw-up. Plus I was sympathetic to Dorothy—she'd accidentally overdosed. My mother puked as a ritual.

I was surprised you could throw up that much. I tried to help Dorothy—holding her hair as she hung over the toilet. Just when I'd think she was soothed and calmed down, she'd hurl again.

I was okay with it.

I wanted to nurture her.

Later, we sat outside on Dorothy's porch steps. She inhaled fresh air and cocooned herself snuggly in her blanket.

Dorothy lit up a cigarette and offered the pack to me. Of course, anything Dorothy suggested was good. I accepted her offer and she lit me up. I coughed a bit on the first inhale.

"Sorry," she said.

I wasn't sure what she was referring to.

"No, I'm cool," I replied to whatever she was sorry about.

"Thanks for helping me back there."

"That's okay."

She was still drunk. "No, you held my head and everything. That was really sweet."

Her mood shifted to serious as she dragged on her cigarette. "Oh, Tim, I have really fucked up."

Dorothy had to spill. I listened intently.

"My husband is not Gene's father. And he knows it on some level, but he married me anyway. And now I've met Peter, and at first, he was so wonderful, and he liked Gene and…"

"So what happened?"

"We had a fight. Peter hit me."

I went to full alert, ready to kill. "He hit you?"

"Slapped me," she clarified.

The line of demarcation wasn't important. Anyone who lifted a finger against Dorothy deserved to die in my opinion, no matter what the circumstances. I put an arm around her and pulled her close. She was rickety. Shivering a little.

She moved her face next to mine. "You're gonna make someone a nice husband someday."

"I could be your husband," I offered.

Even I knew how idiotic that sounded, but I was desperate to prove myself to her. I tried to pawn it off as a joke, but she was touched.

"Aww. You're so innocent."

She pecked me on the lips. I was stunned by the kiss. She had the most luscious lips you could imagine. And even though she'd been throwing up and smoking cigarettes, her breath remained amazingly cool and exciting.

"I'm going to come find you when I'm twenty-one," I declared.

She shook her head and exhaled. "No, you won't. But that's sweet of you to say."

She put a hand against my face and softly brushed my cheek. I felt my heart pound. A yearning stirred between my legs.

"You have such beautiful eyes, Tim."

She kissed me again. Really kissed me. A long kiss. A really good one.

She pulled away. "Okay. This has to stop." She laughed nervously. "Yikes, what am I doing?" She stood up and said, "Okay, you have to go now."

I stood up, not sure what I'd done to break up the party. "I told my mother I was spending the night."

"I'm sorry, but you can't stay here tonight."

She spun around and went inside, leaving me on my own. What the hell.

I stood there like a wax dummy trying to figure out why she was mad at me.

She popped the door and stuck her head out. "Why are you still here?"

"Because I don't want to go home. Why can't I stay here? I won't bother you."

The look in her eyes said she knew that was true. She opened the door wide and motioned me in.

"It's only because you told me your mother's a bitch."

"I appreciate it," I said as I edged past her toward the couch and sat down.

She went to her stereo and put on side one of *The White Album*, being careful to lower the volume before the music kicked in so it wouldn't wake Gene.

She made a deliberate path to the cabinet where she kept the liquor. After rooting around, she came over cradling an open bottle of Bacardi. "Hair of the dog. Rum and Coke, anyone?"

I nodded yes. Of course. Who was she kidding?

She made us both a drink. By the time *Ob-La-Di, Ob-La-Da* made the rounds, I was feeling the buzz and by the time I heard the haunting voice of John Lennon singing "She's not a girl who misses much," I was downright dizzy.

I faded out.

Dorothy flipped the album and it woke me.

I stood up and sat right back down. The rum and Coke had found its mark.

Dorothy laughed, but was a little concerned at the same time. "Tim, are you okay?"

I was reeling, eyes rolling back in my head. She came over and sat beside me, put a gentle hand on my shoulder. "Hey, hon. Really. Do you feel alright?"

Actually I did. I was *flying* on this one cocktail that had hit me like a hammer. "Are you kidding? I feel *great*."

As a matter of fact, I felt so great, I threw myself at her. Tried to steal a kiss. And she kind of half-let me. I hung there, suspended, standing my ground. She surprised the hell out of me by not retreating and kissed me full on the mouth with her luscious wet and cool rum and Coca-Cola lips. Her tongue went in my mouth and mine into hers. My hands wandered and she let them, pushing them into places she thought they should be. This was all new territory for me.

The kissing ran the gamut from moist caressing to lips pressed to the point of pain. A gnashing of faces with dueling tongues. It was hot. She undid the top two buttons of her blouse to show off some cleavage and rolled over on top to straddle me. Her thighs were warm. She didn't shy away from my rock hard boner. While she kissed me on the mouth, she did a slow dry rub up and down with her breasts pressed against my chest.

"How are you doing, Tim?" she whispered playfully. She rubbed some more. This was something straight out of *Overtime* even though we both still had all our clothes on.

A car drove in, followed by a door slam.

Dorothy was off me in a split-second, in survival mode. I leapt up and fell backwards into the recliner, pulling my shirt down in front of a bulge I could only hope to disguise.

"It's my husband," Dorothy announced as she backed up from the blinds. She lit a cigarette to calm herself. "Christ, I never know when this idiot is going to show up."

Dorothy took a seat on the couch right as Jim let himself in. He was an instant third wheel.

"What's goin' on?" he asked goofily.

"Quiet," Dorothy warned. "Gene's down."

"Sorry," he apologized in a whisper.

Jim stood awkwardly waiting for an invitation to sit and join us, but it didn't come, so after a few painfully awkward moments, he tip-toed into the room. He took each step with a look of expected reprisal. Dorothy did nothing but coldly inhale and exhale.

The phone rang. Dorothy shot a look and said, "Who the hell is calling at this hour?" She reached over and picked up.

We all heard squawking coming from the earpiece. Dorothy recoiled and held the handset an inch away from her ear. "I'll send him right over. Sorry."

Dorothy put the phone down. "What the fuck." She looked over at me. "Your mother really is an asshole. Just hung up in my ear."

"You don't have to tell me," I replied.

"You have to go home right away she said."

I rolled my eyes.

"Yeah, I know," she sympathized. "Well, I don't need her callin' the cops on me or something."

I agreed. I just didn't know if I could stand up without my bulge giving me away.

She took a deep drag on her smoke. "I guess you need to get goin', Tim."

I stood up, being careful to maneuver myself around Jim so he didn't notice the hard-on that would not subside.

I made it out their door flashing a peace sign behind me as a distraction.

Stitches

By the time I walked the 20 or so steps around to my trailer, my mother had passed out on her bed with all her clothes on. Once she'd made it that far, she usually would not move much until morning. She'd brought her puke bucket along, so I figured she was in for the night.

I was hungry, so I made the mistake of going into the kitchen thinking I might find some morsel in the fridge. There was nothing but a solitary bottle of her beloved Moxie and a plastic pitcher of bright green Kool-Aid. I tasted the Kool-Aid straight from the container. She hadn't added sugar to it, probably because we didn't have any. Or maybe she forgot to put it in because she was drunk.

I opened up the cupboard. There were a couple of cans of Campbell's soup. Both were Cream of Chicken. Good enough.

I snagged a can and pulled out our catch-all kitchen drawer. I had to paw around, but I uncovered the can-opener. It was a cheapie and the lids rarely came off completely no matter how much muscle you put into it. This time was no different. I forced the clumsy opener around the inside rim and the lid refused to separate on the last inch. I grabbed a butter knife to circle underneath the sharp metal and force the lid up.

This particular lid was being temperamental. With the butter knife wedged up under the lid, I used a thumb to get underneath and apply more leverage. That's when the can slipped out of my grip and I ran the top half of my left thumb horizontally into the sharp metal. To the bone.

At first it didn't bleed. I looked at the wound and the wound looked back at me with the same register of shock. *Then* it bled. A lot. The nerve endings kicked in. Motherfucker, that smarted.

I ran some lukewarm water in the sink and put my thumb under it. Ribbons of bright red blood ran freely as I swallowed the urge to yell out. Each time I took my thumb out and examined the damage, blood flowed so extensively, I couldn't see the actual cut. I rinsed it again and pulled the skin apart while the water flushed the area. I saw the white bone exposed and my knees got wobbly. Okay, this was serious. I needed to see a doctor.

My mother was passed out and we didn't have a car anyway, so what good was she? That was a step I could bypass. I wrapped my thumb tightly in a paper towel and walked straight out of my trailer and over to Dorothy's. I kicked lightly against the bottom of her door with my sneaker.

Jim opened the door. His eyes went right to my bound up thumb and he ushered me in.

"I think I need to go to the doctor," I said, maintaining an even demeanor although I felt like fainting.

"What happened to you?" Jim asked.

"I cut myself on a soup can lid."

Dorothy got up and led me to the kitchen where she held my injured hand over the sink. Jim came in and watched while she gingerly unwrapped the paper towel. The skin on either side of the cut was drained white.

Dorothy caved back. "Damn." She turned to Jim. "He needs to go to the emergency room. Now."

Jim stepped up. "I'll take him."

"You or me," Dorothy said.

"No, I'll do it," Jim insisted.

He turned to me.

"Let's go."

The drive to the hospital was short. Less than ten minutes. Jim gave me a piece of gum to cover up the alcohol on my breath. I don't remember talking much. I was at least mildly in shock and Jim understood that which was why he didn't engage me in conversation except to ask "Are you alright?" repeatedly.

At the emergency room, they took me in quickly. I have no idea how any of the paperwork was accomplished or how Jim was able to act as my guardian, but they worked on me. The fact that my mother was employed in the system as a nurse might've greased the skids. Maybe it was all off the books. Jim might've even paid the bill. I was spared the details.

I sat in a chair with my arm propped up on an adjacent stainless steel table while a doctor assisted by a nurse worked on me. First, the doctor swabbed the laceration with a brownish liquid, then brandished a needle loaded with anesthetic. He injected in a couple of places on either side of the gash and apologized when I winced.

"This is going to take a few," he said under his breath to the nurse.

I watched him sew each stitch. It was an odd feeling to watch hooks thread through my numb skin and tug.

Jim stayed in the room the whole time.

That meant something to me.

On the way home, Jim asked if I was hungry. You bet. Starving. We swung by the Dairy Queen.

We ate in the car. Flame-broiled cheeseburgers with onion rings, milk shakes, and hot chocolate ice cream sundaes. Jim was worried if I was okay. I told him I was. He laughed when I got ketchup all over one side of my mouth.

When we got back to my mother's trailer, it was almost 9 PM. Jim decided to follow me in.

I heard my mother snoring in her bedroom as soon as we stepped inside. Jim side-stepped around me and took a few steps up the hallway to peek into my mother's room.

He was pissed. "Ma'am," he called out.

The snores got louder.

So did Jim. "Ma'am!"

She didn't move. I didn't expect her to.

"Ma'am, your son has been injured and taken to the hospital and needs to be monitored after being treated. Ma'am, can you hear me?"

My mother sawed out a reply.

Jim tucked his shirt tighter into his pants and snorted in disgust. "Okay, Ma'am, here's the deal, and I hope you can hear me. I'm taking Tim to stay at our place. You can call me when you are able."

Jim grabbed my arm. "C'mon, you're staying with us."

And I went.

"Six stitches," I boasted.

"Damn," Dorothy sympathized.

"His mother's a bitch," Jim declared.

Dorothy agreed. "Tell me about it."

Jim sat upright in his chair and engaged me like a buddy. "You want a belt?"

"Sure." Once again, I was digging the grown-up atmosphere.

For some reason, Dorothy was cautious. "Jim. You think this is a good idea?"

Jim popped up, grabbed a bottle of Seagrams 7 out of their cabinet, and swished back into the room. "He's safe, he's not behind the wheel of a car, and he's not under the care of his bitch mother."

I cheered that sentiment with the first potent cocktail Jim slipped my way.

I don't remember how many drinks I had.

I woke up in the dark lying on my side wearing nothing but my underwear. They'd put me on their sleeper sofa.

It was deep night stillness and I felt queasy. I could tell getting up would be a bad option, so I didn't move after my eyelids fluttered open. I stared into the darkness, letting my pupils adjust.

I felt a presence behind me, but didn't dare face it. Don't ask me why, I was petrified. Thick tension hung stagnantly in the air. An arm casually made its way across my ribs and down in front of me, resting dangerously close to my equipment.

"You okay?" a voice asked. Jim's voice.

"I feel a little sick," I said.

"Really?" he said with coiled snake concern.

He stroked my stomach in small circles with the palm of his hand.

"Right in here? Is this where you don't feel good?"

And then his hand went lower and brushed against my dick.

My survival mechanism kicked in, full throttle. I sprung up off the couch and vaulted unnaturally to their picture window, peeling the blinds back to look over at my trailer. "I need to go home," I announced.

Jim inched closer on the sleeper. "You don't have to go. You could make yourself a sandwich or something."

Fuck this pervert. I hastily struggled to get my clothes on. "No, I think I better get home."

"How's that thumb feeling? Okay?"

"It's fine." Actually, it was thumping like a motherfucker.

"You want another drink?" he offered.

I was adamant. "No, I need to go home."

Jim shrugged and grinned his toothy grin, which looked extra creepy in the semi-dark. "Oh, okay, well, go home then."

I went back to my mother's louder than normal log cutting. The devil I knew was better than the one I didn't know.

I finally got to sleep an hour later.

I didn't tell anyone what happened.

Not even Elvis.

Smegma

Elvis and I waited for the bus. The good, the bad, and the ugly. Elvis had insulated me for so long, I'd gotten cocky. Stupidly so.

I puffed up and checked with Elvis to catch his eye. He shook his head in disapproval. But you couldn't tell me anything. Like I said, I'd gotten cocky.

"Hey, Moosie."

He seemed surprised I would address him. "What?"

"You ever heard of smegma?" I asked.

"Why? Should I?"

Newfound knowledge combined with my inability to keep my mouth shut plagued me even then. I couldn't resist.

"Yeah, you should know what it is because it's what you are. Smegma."

I laughed in the face of Moosie's ignorance and he clearly was not amused. When I looked over, Elvis cracked a smile, but he also had a look in his eye of "Hey, it's your funeral."

Moosie didn't like someone having the upper hand. He could barely contain his rage. So of course I had to lay it on extra thick. I zeroed in on his contorted face.

"Smegma. What is it?"

During third period study hall, I saw Moosie wrestling with an unabridged dictionary in the school library. I couldn't believe he found it on his own. He must have asked someone.

I could tell when he located the mystery word on the page.

His face changed and not in a good way.

At the end of the school day, Elvis and I waited in the school parking lot for the bus. Moosie wrenched some kids out of his way to face off with me. I could already feel my mouth about to get me in trouble again.

I led off with, "Hey, smegma. What's up?"

Moosie was a ball of kinetic energy. Sizzling. "You fucker. I looked that up."

"Who read it to you?" Excellent comeback. I was proud of myself.

He balled his fists. "There's gonna come a day."

"And what?" I was definitely feeling my oats.

"There'll come a day when you don't have your big bodyguard around."

Elvis turned to Moosie. "Back off, stupid."

Moosie shut his mouth, but when he looked at me, he wanted me dead.

On the way home, Elvis and I sat in the middle section of the bus. At the back, Moosie and his friends terrorized little grade-schoolers.

Elvis angled into me. "You need to start pickin' your battles and work on keepin' your mouth shut."

I was full of myself. "Why?"

"Cause he's right. There will come a day."

On some level, I knew he was right, and on another level, I was mad at him for sticking a pin in my balloon.

The following afternoon, I was given permission to leave school early. After I'd complained three or four times that my teeth hurt, my mother arranged for me to visit a dentist. Even though the government paid for most of the visit because of her low-income status, my mother didn't want to send me because she knew it was going to cost her money. Like that mattered. I knew my mother well enough to know she'd never pay her share anyway.

It was my first visit to a dentist. Ever. The doctor's office wasn't far from the school and my mother arranged for Bill to pick me up afterwards since I wouldn't be done in time to make the bus home.

The assistant was cute as a button, especially in her whites. She spoke in soothing tones.

The dentist was a dick. I heard him mutter under his breath that he was "tired of taking on charity cases." Like it was my fault my mother was a loser.

His demeanor went from bad to worse once he took a look inside my mouth. He did a double-take and invited his assistant to take a gander.

He shook his head in disgust as he poked around with a stainless steel hook. "Get a mirror over here so he can see this." Uh-oh. That didn't sound good. She wheeled an overhead mirror into place so it reflected back from the circular small mirror he was tapping around inside my mouth.

He had hairy coarse hands. "Whatever you do, don't bite me," he warned as he forced my mouth open more than I thought was possible. He indicated the mirror above my head. "Can you see in there?" I nodded yes, as much as I could. He had me pinned down solid.

Using the hook, he stuck it in 9 of my teeth, calling out tooth numbers for each one—4 on the top, 5 on the bottom—mostly back teeth with special attention paid to the molars.

Pulling back slightly, he said, "Every tooth I just touched has a major cavity. Not only that, you need a thorough cleaning before I can even start."

He poked the mirror back in my mouth and reflected the backs of my top front teeth. "You see that?"

"Uh-hmm." I know my eyes had to be wide because this guy was making me nervous as hell.

"You know what that buildup is?"

I shook my head no as much as he'd let me.

"That's a calculus bridge. Plaque buildup. That means you're not brushing right."

I'd been given a new toothbrush every couple of years, but I'd never been shown how to work it, so the bad news wasn't completely unexpected. Still, I thought overall I'd done well to figure it out by myself, but apparently I'd missed some spots.

He averted his eyes to telegraph to his assistant the last thing in the world he wanted to do was work on me. "I've got the rest of the afternoon blocked out, so we can do the cleaning today and let's knock out several fillings. We'll have to set up another appointment to do the rest."

The girl in whites wheeled over a tray of instruments.

He sat to my right and leaned in close. "Okay, let's get this over with. We'll have to use a hammer and chisel to get some of this off."

And that's exactly what it felt like. I rinsed mouthfuls of blood into the spittoon between gagging on my own fluids. When he was done, my teeth felt loose. It was a painful experience and that was just the warm-up.

The Novocain needles were huge and scary. He had the assistant load six syringes. She lined them up one by one on a white towel draped over the tray. When he said, "Hold still, 'cause this is going to get a little sticky," I knew that was code for "You're not going to like this part." Finesse was not this idiot's strong suit. He might as well have hurled the syringes into my mouth from the other side of the room.

He got pissed when one of my teeth wasn't fully numb. I jerked in the chair when the drilling got a bit intense. Rather than give me another shot, he encouraged me to swallow the pain because it would take too long to administer more anesthetic.

When he was done, he went to the sink and washed his hands.

The assistant wiped the corners of my frozen mouth and helped me out of the chair.

I felt the sides of my numb face.

The assistant smiled. "Yeah, feels funny, huh? Don't worry, it'll wear off in a couple of hours. Just don't drink anything too hot right away and don't eat until dinner. You want those fillings to set right."

As the dentist dried his hands, he said, "Maybe you'll pay more attention to taking care of your teeth from now on."

I wanted to punch this fucker.

Pink Belly

The next morning at the bus stop, a series of events kicked off that solidified something in my mind. Fortunes can indeed turn on a dime. The situation began with me on top.

Moosie pushed the smallest girl at the bus stop, then knocked the books out of her arms. God, didn't he ever get tired of his own act?

I asserted myself. "Hey. Smegma. Pick on someone your own size. Oh, wait, there's no one else as small as you, is there?"

"I told you," he threatened as he formed a fist.

I pushed right back. "Told me what, smegma?"

Moosie's blood boiled. "Stop calling me that."

"Or what?"

It's a good thing you can't predict your future because if I'd known how this day was going to turn out, I might have chosen my words more carefully.

I changed out of my gym clothes. Any time I spent in the isolation of the school locker room was never good. I was always vulnerable in Phys Ed, but up till this point, the threat of Elvis waiting at the bus stop had been enough to keep the trolls at bay.

But I'd crossed a line that morning while waiting for the bus. Richard and Elwood came around a wall of lockers and boxed me in. Moosie appeared with a towel draped around his neck and centered himself between his henchmen to square off with me.

"I could pound you right here," he said. "But it's better if you don't know when it's coming. And it is coming, welfare boy."

Moosie unwrapped the towel from around his neck and coiled one end around his right hand. "I didn't appreciate that smegma bullshit, and if you ever call me that again, consider yourself dead."

As a period at the end of his sentence, he snapped his towel right between my legs. It stung like a sonofabitch. And kept stinging. Intensifying. I thought I was going to heave. I felt my anger rising exponentially. I clenched my fists to stay grounded.

Elwood and Richard got a charge out of my tough-guy persona.

Moosie got up in my face. "Just try it, peckerhead. You'll be sorry you ever did." He swiftly grabbed hold of one of my nipples and twisted it. "Tittie-twister."

I jumped back with my arms up in self-defense. Moosie scoffed at the picture. "Illya Kuryakin. Yeah. Right."

Moosie went for my other nipple, but I moved away in time. He snapped me in the legs with his towel.

Moosie turned to Richard and Elwood and said, "C'mon. Let's get away from this homo." Before leaving, he drove his threat home. "See you at the bus stop. We'll be there every day waiting for you. Till it's your day. Homo."

Moosie took a swipe at my face, but I ducked and he missed me.

"Two for flinching," he crowed.

Richard grabbed me and I spat out, "Let me go, dick!"

He secured my arm so Moosie could punch me. "It's fuckin' *Richard* and I already told you that."

I was purple with rage. "I forgot."

Moosie moved closer. "You ever watch The Three Stooges?"

Without any warning, he poked me straight in the eyes. I saw stars.

"That's for bein' too smart," Moosie observed as he grabbed my upper arm and delivered two vicious blows.

"Ahh, you fucker!" I yelled at him as I struggled to see. "Get your fuckin' hands off me!"

Moosie had regained the upper hand. He stuck his chest out. "Or what?"

I tried to free myself and got elbowed into a wall of lockers.

"What a pussy," Moosie said derisively as he signaled his boys to back off.

I shook myself out defiantly. Moosie chuckled at my defeat. As they left, his final insult echoed in the locker room.

"See you around, Smegma."

I cornered Elvis at his locker between classes. "Moosie and his friends came after me in Phys Ed."

This didn't cut any slack with Elvis. "Yeah, no shit. I told you to keep your damned mouth shut."

"I need to go out a different exit or something."

Elvis waved off my suggestion. "No, I'll walk you out. It's cool."

Fate delivered a blow to my escape plan and altered my destiny an hour later right before the final bell. I had my getaway mapped out, my meeting point with Elvis synchronized.

My spinster home room teacher Miss Barter finished up erasing the blackboard.

Across the aisle from me, Moosie begged my attention. Once our eyes met, he took his pencil—his metaphor for me—and held it with both hands. Before he snapped it, he mouthed the words, "This is you."

Moosie cracked the pencil and it splintered in two. He smiled "you're next" at me.

What a little rodent. Well, I had protection, so fuck him.

Miss Barter set the eraser down in the chalk tray and faced the class. "I need a volunteer to clean the blackboards and the erasers."

No hands went up. She pointed to me. "Timothy?"

I broke into an immediate sweat. "No, I can't," I fumbled.

"Why not?" she demanded.

"I'm allergic to chalk dust," I lied. Wow. Good save. Pulled that out of my ass. I was kind of proud of myself for just coming up with that on the fly.

To my amazement, she backed right off without challenging me. "Oh, alright. Sorry." She scanned the room for a suitable replacement. "Let's see," she thought out loud as she looked over the faces in the room. Trust me, nobody wanted this gig.

Moosie piped up. "Timmy's not allergic to chalk dust. He's lying."

He was telling the truth. I was lying. But he didn't know that. He took a gamble and it paid off.

Miss Barter reverted back to me. "Timothy, is that true?"

I could have lied again. After all, I was pretty good at it. But as a kid, I thought I'd go to hell if I lied in answer to a teacher's direct question. I fessed up. "Yes, it's true."

As the second-hand crept up to the bell ringing, Miss Barter looked me straight in the eye and provided concrete direction. "Please stay after class."

I was utterly beat down. In the hole. "Yes, ma'am."

The bell rang and the students filed out of the room as fast as they could.

Miss Barter called out "No running!" over the chaotic stampede.

Once the students were gone, she walked slowly with purpose to the desk in front of mine and sat down sideways so she could address me one-on-one.

I couldn't meet her gaze. I literally hung my head. I was too mixed up—humiliation fueling guilt, flavored with a dash of "I'm going to get my ass beat as soon as I leave this room."

She didn't say anything for a few seconds. It was like centuries ticking by. Finally, "Look at me."

It was difficult, but I did.

"Why did you lie to me?" she asked. I could tell she was really interested in the answer. She wasn't angry, she was hurt, which is a worse thing to contend with.

I felt myself well up. God, I hated my weakness, my inability to stand up to anything.

I didn't answer her right away. I was too busy trying to stop the tears that wanted to burn their way down my face.

She cut me no slack. She wasn't going to let me off without answering. "Hmm?" she persisted. "Why did you do that?"

To avoid an ass beating. That's what I wanted to tell her.

I had no answer for lying that would be acceptable. I shrugged my shoulders and mumbled, "I just did, I don't know why."

She rose in slow motion and hovered over my desk in a matronly way. She saw this as a teachable moment. "Do you know why I believed you?"

I shook my head no.

"Do you know why I don't clean the blackboards myself?"

I shook my head no a second time.

"It's not because I'm lazy," she continued. "I just can't. I'm allergic to chalk dust. And since I suffer from that allergy, when you told me you did too, I understood why you couldn't do it."

God. It wasn't like I already didn't feel like a piece of shit for lying to her. Now she had to ice the cake.

"There was no reason to lie to me," she scolded. "I would never lie to *you*. Frankly, I'm very surprised, Timothy."

I couldn't control the waterworks. Tears spilled down my cheeks, one by one. She knew she had me. I felt the next barb coming, but I hoped she wouldn't let that arrow fly. She did anyway.

"Worst of all, I'm very disappointed in you."

Ahh, dammit! The D word. Put a knife through my heart. I would rather she'd dragged me behind a car than tell me she was disappointed in me.

And to sum it all up, with a final twist of the dagger, she put the final nail in the coffin. "Disappointed," she said. She'd condensed everything into that one word and used it twice to great effect.

Having made her indelible impression, she told me to get to work. I did as I was told. I hung the top half of my body out a window and clapped erasers together to clear the chalk dust. Using a moist cloth, I wiped the chalk residue from the dark green blackboards and finished by wiping down the chalk rails. When I was done, she didn't say anything—just nodded her approval of my work and acknowledged I could leave.

I prayed that Elvis had hung back and waited where I could find him.

The hallways were empty. Lifelessly silent.

I approached my locker, constantly checking both ways. I ditched the books I didn't need for homework and clanged my locker shut. I spun the combo dial and got on my way.

It was eerie in the corridors when no one was around. As I rounded a corner into the last hallway I needed to traverse to get outside, they stood waiting for me.

Richard and Elwood both grabbed an arm and lifted me off the floor.

"Someone's waiting to see you," Richard sneered.

They dragged me out one of the side doors and down the steps to a small clearing surrounded by bushes.

From this vantage point, I could see the school bus stop down below at the bottom of the hill. A worried Elvis paced as he watched for me.

Moosie popped out of the bushes. "Well, look what we have here. Smegma. Homo welfare boy. Illya Kuryakin… except without his big fat bodyguard."

I pulled with all my might to break free, but I wasn't going anywhere.

Moosie's eyes were darker than normal. "So now we get to see how you do when you have to fight your own battles."

I clutched my school books in front of me as some kind of pussy barrier. Moosie bashed them out of my arms to the ground with a single swipe. He bent over, picked up my math book, and found some loose-leaf notebook pages folded up inside—my half-completed homework. He held up the papers. "What's this? Some homework?"

Moosie chucked my efforts to the winds and raggedly ripped out a big hunk of the book's center. He tossed the torn pages over his shoulder and said, "You better remember to read that chapter later tonight." He laughed and Frisbee'd what was left of my book into the bushes.

Moosie kicked the rest of my books out of the way to clear the ground at his feet. He checked in with Richard and Elwood and indicated the spot in front of him. "Put him right here."

Richard and Elwood threw me on the grass at Moosie's feet.

I heard him say, "Okay. Hold him down."

Richard and Elwood each took a side, holding down my arms and legs as if they were going to draw and quarter me. Grinning like a crazed Jack Nicholson, Moosie straddled me and slowly lowered himself down to sit on my stomach like a rodeo cowboy settling on a bull before the gate flies open.

Moosie ripped my shirt open down the front to expose my chest and roughly twisted my nipples. I bucked and he reached around and nailed me in the privates.

"Pink belly!" Elwood suggested.

This played right into Moosie's plan. "Excellent suggestion!"

Moosie glowered at me and poked my sternum with a stiff index finger. "You know what a pink belly is?" He poked my sternum harder. "You feel this bone right here?"

I practically begged. "Get off me, Moosie."

He smiled as he rolled up his sleeves. "I'm not done with you yet, welfare kid."

He balled up a fist and pounded his knuckles repeatedly against my sternum. He rapped with a vengeance. As I struggled, Richard and Elwood got in some licks on my arms and legs.

It was unrelenting. I couldn't help but cry. Moosie cracked me across the face. "Fuckin' cunt. You think it's funny calling me smegma? Well, who's smegma now?"

He hocked up a big lunger in his throat and oozed a nasty mass of phlegm between his lips. It dangled over my head as I stretched my neck to avoid the inevitable. He cupped my face to steady it so his spit could fall into my mouth. I choked. Spluttered.

He threw a handful of dirt in my eyes, jumped up while I was writhing around, and kicked me straight in the balls. The pain and nausea took a second or two to register.

Half-digested food tried to make its way up my throat, but I swallowed it back down. I squirmed to get up, but Moosie's big oafs had me in an iron grip.

"Hold him!" Moosie ordered.

And then the *coup de grâce*. Moosie undid his fly, pulled his dick out, and pissed on me. I remember it all going quiet during this twenty seconds of absolute humiliation.

Moosie zipped up. "Okay. Let him go."

Richard and Elwood both got in a final jab before letting me up.

I was seeing red.

Reading my mind, Moosie cautioned me. "And don't think about cryin' to your fat friend. He tries anything with us and we'll be on you every fuckin' day of the week."

I pulled my ripped shirt closed and stumbled my way down to the bus stop to stand behind my attackers. Elvis silently joined me at my side. The trio of bullies made faces at Elvis as they hopped up onto the bus.

Elvis took in my battered and bruised appearance. "What the hell happened to you?"

On the bus, I curled into myself.

Elvis had been worried. "I waited forever and you didn't show up."

Using a sleeve, I wiped clear mucus from my upper lip and stared out the window.

Elvis sighed. "Man, I shoulda knew something was up because I didn't see Moosie or those other two fuckers hangin' around down here. I shoulda come to look for ya."

Elvis's wheels were spinning. He'd made a decision in his head. I just didn't know it yet. And that could go either way with as much potential for bad as good.

When we reached our stop, Elvis calmly got off first and waited for Moosie and his entourage.

As I hopped off, I saw the focus in Elvis's eyes. Something was about to go down. Under my breath, I said, "Let's just forget about it."

Elvis was vehement. "No." Case closed.

Moosie, backed up by Richard and Elwood, stepped off the bus. Elvis glared at them as they brushed past us and walked off down the sidewalk.

Moosie felt the heat on the back of his neck and spun around to face off. "What?"

That was all Elvis needed. He steamrolled those punks.

Richard got it first. Elvis clocked him right between the eyes and Richard went down like a ton of bricks.

Moosie lurched toward Elvis, but Elvis collared him before Moosie could do any damage. Elvis threw Moosie like a used paper cup.

Elwood moved in and Elvis manhandled him backward into a tree.

Moosie made a dash to escape, but Elvis lunged and nabbed him.

Richard recovered and t-boned Elvis who feinted back, tripping over the curb into the street.

A car sped by, barely missing my big friend.

Even the perpetrators looked scared at the near miss.

Elvis regained his footing and stomped back onto the sidewalk.

"Holy shit!" Elwood yelped.

"Run!" Moosie wailed.

And they did.

Peter

Dorothy mothered me. After mixing me a serious no bullshit cocktail, she cracked a tray of ice cubes and folded them inside a hand towel. She made me lie down on her couch and hold the ice pack against my bright pink breast bone. She winced when she got a good look at it.

Elvis sat nearby with little Gene propped up on one knee.

Dorothy sat down, lit a cigarette, and tossed the pack to Elvis.

She exhaled. "You talk to your mother about this?"

"Are you kidding?" I asked in disbelief. "The only thing she'd be pissed about is having to replace a school book."

Elvis confirmed. "Yeah, I don't think talking to her would really help the situation. You know, knowing her."

Dorothy was upset. "You think I should go to the school or something?"

I objected right away. "Oh, hell, no."

Elvis seconded my sentiment with a nod. "Yeah, that probably wouldn't be good in the long run."

Dorothy shook her head. "Yeah, well…I'm sorry." She got up, parked her cigarette in the ashtray, and went out to the kitchen. She called out to the living room. "Darrell, did you want a drink?"

Elvis declined.

"Well, I think I'll have one," she said as she came back in with a glass of ice. She went to the liquor cabinet, splashed a couple of fingers of Bacardi into her tumbler, and topped it off with fizzing Coke.

A loud knock sounded at the door. More knocks came in rapid succession. Aggressive knocks.

Dorothy set her drink down and cautiously approached the door.

Uneasiness bled into the room.

I moved my ice pack away and sat up straight. I was quite a sight with my torn shirt and my puny pink chest.

Dorothy hesitated at the door. She took a step closer and it banged open.

Dorothy jumped back.

Peter frothed in. Raging drunk. Fuse burning.

He beamed unnaturally as he surveyed the room. "Oh, havin' a party!" he observed with a noticeable slur.

He cornered Dorothy and eyed Elvis and me like he'd never met us before. "How old are these boys?"

"We're old enough," I heard myself spout off.

Peter tried to center on me, but he had trouble locking in. "Who's talkin' over there?" he wondered out loud.

Gene fussed and began to cry.

Dorothy looked and sounded worried. "Peter, you need to go. Please."

Without ceremony, he batted a floor lamp over, crashing it to the floor. Dorothy leapt back with a yelp.

Peter was defiant. "Nobody tells me when I need to go!"

Gene cried louder. Elvis tried to settle him.

Peter shook a fist at Elvis. "Shut up! Shut it! That fuckin' kid better shut its mouth!"

Gene reciprocated with unrestrained screaming.

Peter advanced on Elvis and Gene. Dorothy intercepted to diffuse the situation. "Peter! Stop it!"

I found myself levitating off the couch. "Hey!"

Peter stopped in his tracks and faced me when he saw me stand up. "Just who in the fuck did you think you're talking to?"

I quaked in my boots, but stood my ground.

Dorothy scooped Gene out of Elvis's arms and ran to the adjoining dining room space. It gave her some distance, but no protection to speak of.

Peter whipped around. "I see where you are!"

Dorothy pleaded. "Peter, just go. You're scaring us."

He reveled in that notion and focused on Elvis in the recliner.

"Who are you?"

"None of your business," Elvis fired back.

Elvis was bold. He didn't take any shit. I had to give him that.

Peter couldn't believe his ears. "I beg your pardon?"

Standoff.

Elvis didn't back down. Instead, he rose to a standing position, and even though Peter was in much better shape, I could tell he was freaked out by the overall height/weight disadvantage. Peter blinked and took a step back.

Elvis reiterated. "I said…it's none of your business."

Peter went after Dorothy and Gene.

Dorothy shielded Gene and shouted angrily, "Peter, don't!"

Peter was determined to show he was the master. He moved on her, bellowing, "You don't walk out on me!"

Elvis stepped in front of Peter. Dorothy grabbed the phone and shakily dialed 0 with one hand to get the operator.

Peter side-stepped and grabbed the receiver off the table. He yanked the handset out of Dorothy's hands and pulled the connecting wires out of the wall simultaneously. "What are you doing, bitch?" Peter thundered.

And then he went to hit her.

His mistake. Elvis reared up like a grizzly and landed a thick meaty fist against the side of Peter's head. It caught him right on the jaw line and Peter was clearly knocked for a loop. Hurt.

Peter careened into a chair and steadied himself.

"You nasty fat sonofabitch!"

Elvis apparently didn't appreciate the insult. Plus Peter made his second big mistake of the evening when he attempted another lunge at Dorothy. When Elvis's fist came around the corner and telephone-poled into Peter's left eye, it surprised everyone. When my big friend made contact, the power behind his punch was unmistakable. Peter visibly rocked in place, searching desperately for balance. As his eyes rolled around in his head, Peter's stunned expression corkscrewed into a devil from hell and he doubled up his fists in retaliation.

Peter wanted to take the fight to the next level so he could whip Elvis's ass in front of us. Sure, Elvis was huge, but Peter was muscular and if he ran around the fat kid enough times, he could eventually wear Elvis down. Elvis figured out Peter's plans about a second before Peter had finalized them.

Without hesitation, Elvis brought in a roundhouse right and clocked Peter right above his already swelling eye. Time froze for an instant and before Peter could fully catalog the punch, Elvis landed another one. This time it was a bit lower. We heard Peter's eye socket crack. He had to be seeing stars.

Peter reeled off into the wall and slid partly down, cupping his wounds with his hands. "Oww! Fuck!" he yelled. "Sonofabitch! I'll get you!" he threatened as he straightened up. He shook a finger at Elvis. "I will fucking get you!"

I had to hand it to Peter. This fucker had the gift of gab.

Elvis lumbered forward to deliver another salvo and Peter cut his losses. He made tracks outside and hot-rodded his pick-up out of her driveway like it was stolen. Gone.

Elvis made sure Peter was gone, then closed the door and addressed Dorothy.

"You okay?"

Dorothy calmed Gene and shook her head yes, but she was far from okay.

Elvis looked over at me. "How about you?"

"Yeah, I'm fine," I groused.

Elvis snickered like nothing had happened and shook his hand out. "Damn, that hurt a little."

Dorothy shook uncontrollably as she fumbled to twist the flimsy door knob lock into place. Like somehow that half-assed security measure would protect us if Peter returned.

She snatched what was left of her cigarette out of the ashtray and inhaled deeply.

Elvis took Gene from her and spoke reassuringly. "My dad's out of town. I can spend the night if you want."

She exhaled nervously. "Would you mind, Darrell? 'Cause that'd be great."

I wanted to spend the night too, but I couldn't call to ask permission. I resigned myself to spending the night in my own bed and walked around from Dorothy's to my mother's trailer.

Along the way, I fired off Karate moves to combat unseen assailants in the dark. I *was* Illya. Illya Kuryakin. *The Man from U.N.C.L.E.*

Karate kicking my ass off into thin air.

My mother was comatose. Slumped over in her chair. Lifeless. I thought she was dead.

I shook her. "Hey."

No response. I shook her again.

Nothing.

I lifted her head up. She didn't appear to be breathing. My heart pounded. The thing about my mother was she always came back. No matter how tanked she got, you could count on her rising from the dead every time.

I put an ear against her chest. I couldn't hear breathing or a heartbeat. I wasn't sure how to do CPR, but I knew it involved opening and forcing air into her mouth while pinching her nose. I hung over her and mashed her nostrils together with an index finger and a thumb as I lowered my face to hers.

Suddenly, she snorted to life and scared the hell out of me. She waved blindly in the TV's direction. "I was watchin' that!"

As quickly as she'd popped up, she fell out again.

I looked down at her pathetic lot and shook my head. God. Could she be any more of a train wreck?

"Well, keep watchin' it," I said to the four walls as I walked down the hallway to my room and shut the door behind me.

I deflated on my bed. At least I hadn't had to explain the day's events and listen to her corn-hole advice. I laughed to myself derisively.

My mother never even noticed my shirt was ripped down the front.

That was probably a good thing.

Less hell to pay.

All Gone

The next day, I got to school late. Bill and my mother drove me straight to a first-thing-in-the-morning appointment where the dick dentist finished off the rest of my teeth in a two and a half hour marathon session.

Normally I'd see Elvis in passing between classes, but on this day, I didn't. Elvis wasn't there. It was a weird vibe and I didn't know why. Something had shifted in the cosmos. I could feel it.

I skipped part of my lunch period to hang back in home room.

Miss Barter gave me a questioning glare as I sheepishly approached the front of her desk hanging my head.

"Yes, Timothy."

Keeping my head down, I handed over my mutilated math book.

She opened it in a state of mild horror.

"What happened?"

"I dropped it and it got run over by a car," I replied with my dentist-deadened tongue.

She stayed frosty. "I see."

I could tell she didn't believe me. But amazingly enough, she didn't pursue any follow-up questions I'd have to bluff my way through.

I raised my head in an effort to pull my dignity together. "How much does it cost to replace it?"

My question took her off guard. She turned official. Went all business on me. "These are used books. Six dollars would probably cover the replacement."

I had over ten bucks in my pocket. I thought it might be more, so I was relieved I had enough to cover the damages and she could see it in my face. I inched closer to her desk and pulled paperboy money from both front pockets. A couple of crumpled ones tumbled out, but most of the bounty that spilled out was change.

She watched me shakily smooth out the bills and line them up next to four dollars in quarters and dimes. I slid the money toward her.

She stared at me up and down. She was good at that. And then this weird thing happened. Her face softened. She looked like somebody totally different. She pushed the money back. "The truth of the matter is these books are being replaced next year."

She regained some formality and pointed to my cash. "Hang on to your money. Put it in a bank."

It struck me that she never intended for me to pay. It was a test. She just wanted to see if I had any measure of integrity.

That singular gesture made a mark on me for the rest of my life.

In homeroom after lunch, I milled around my desk in ignorance.

Moosie swaggered up beside me with a shit-eating smirk on his puss. "So…sorry to hear about your friend."

I was on high alert. "Who?"

Moosie filled in the gap for me. "Fatso."

"His name is Darrell," I said thickly, still numb from the Novocain.

"Yeah, well, I heard he got hit by a car this mornin'."

I felt like I'd been punched. My heart raced. A wave of anger washed over me. "If you did anything to him—"

Moosie hauled off and elbowed me in the ribs.

It caught me off guard. I searched for air, but couldn't catch a breath as I gripped the edge of my desk for support.

"How'd that feel?" he asked as he set up to hit me again.

Another elbow. I still couldn't get my wind, but managed to croak out, "You suck."

Moosie forced me down into my seat.

"Get used to it, carrot-top. The rest of your life ain't worth livin'."

In afternoon classes, I was worthless. Couldn't concentrate. I put my head down on my hands in last period. It was funny how they never made an announcement about Elvis, yet everyone in the school knew he'd been hit by a car. But after that, details were sketchy.

There were rumors it had gone down at the bus stop. I'd heard he'd thrown up after he was hit. Some even heard he was dead.

Nobody knew for sure.

At the end of the school day, I waited at the bus stop for Moosie, Elwood and Richard.

"Hey, smegma," Moosie sneered as they surrounded me.

"What'd you do to Darrell?" I demanded.

Moosie rocked back and forth on his heels. "We didn't touch that big pig. He's just fuckin' clumsy."

They'd picked the wrong day to mess with me. It was a light switch moment in my head. I didn't care about consequences anymore. I stepped toward them with laser beams coming out of my eyes. I could have killed each one of them ten times over. Moosie and his boys were surprised. They instinctively backed off as a group. Noticeably hands off.

That was the first time I'd felt concentrated adult power.

All I'd done was push back with nothing more than a look on my face.

And they flinched.

I jumped off the bus and ran to Steve Oreno's. He'd be straight with me.

I stood at the counter breaking into a sweat. Steve confirmed that my friend had been hit and taken to the hospital. But as far as Steve knew, Elvis was still alive.

I was gasping. My stomach churned.

"I think they pushed him."

Steve tried to calm me. "The cops came around earlier. Nobody saw anything according to them."

"Bullshit. There's no way he just fell into the street."

I turned to leave and Steve said, "Don't do anything stupid, my friend."

"I'm going to see him at the hospital."

Steve offered counsel. "They won't let you visit him— you're not a relative."

"I'm his best friend," I reasoned.

Steve shook his head. "They don't give a shit about that."

I made my way to Elvis's trailer and knocked my knuckles raw. I knew someone was home because there was a construction company pick-up in the driveway.

Elvis's father opened the door. It occurred to me that we'd never actually been introduced, but I recognized him right away from seeing him that one time standing next to Elvis the day they'd moved in.

Instead of inviting me in, his dad stepped outside, forcing me backwards down the steps. The old man was ashen. "What do you want, son?" he asked sternly.

"I'm a friend of Darrell's," I sputtered. "Where is he? Is he okay?"

"He's not—I'm sorry to tell ya—he's not good. He's gonna be in intensive care for a coupla days. Now you go home."

He went inside and tugged the door shut behind him.

A man of few words.

Great.

Dorothy's driveway was empty, but I knocked anyway. Once again, she'd been gone for a couple of days without telling us where she was going. I knocked repeatedly even though I knew no one was home. Finally, I gave up and sat down on her porch to massage my knuckles.

It was getting dark when I heard her engine roar up. An answer to prayer I didn't deserve descended and an angel steered her car into the driveway.

Dorothy led me into her trailer. I was shocked. Except for the stereo and her records, the place was cleaned out. Barren. Her phone had been set down in a corner on the floor. The wires Peter had ripped from the wall had been carefully coiled and placed on top of the handset.

"Are you moving?" I asked, not wanting to know the answer.

Dorothy was all serious, no smiles. "Things are not safe here."

"Where's Gene?" I asked.

"He's at my mother's house in Connecticut."

"Your husband's a homosexual," I heard myself blurt out.

"Excuse me?"

"Jim tried to get with me."

Dorothy didn't say anything initially. Instead, she reached inside her purse and took out a pack of smokes and a lighter. Dorothy inched out a cigarette for herself and offered me one. I took it. She lit hers, then mine.

I could tell Dorothy was really mulling over what I'd said.

"Are you sure?" she asked, avoiding smoke behind a squinted eye.

"Oh, yeah. I'm sure."

"Well, that explains some things."

"It does?"

"Yeah," she exhaled. "Like why he never wanted to have sex with me."

"What do you mean?"

"Honey, in the year and a half since we got married, we've done it a total of eight times and that includes our wedding night, okay?"

I was dumbfounded. "You're kidding."

"No, I'm not," she said matter-of-fact.

Dorothy was being deliberately standoffish and I knew on every level that wasn't good. Logically, I knew this was the moment she was leaving, but emotionally, the thought wasn't making it completely through my thick skull.

Her eyes made a finalizing sweep. "This was my last run. I came back for the stereo and my records."

The gravity weighed in. "What? You mean if I hadn't been here, you would have left without saying goodbye?"

Dorothy didn't answer. She went to the record player, knelt down, and flipped through her albums.

I sat on the floor next to her.

She flicked her ashes on the floor, so I did, too.

Dorothy pulled out *The Mamas and the Papas present The Papas and the Mamas* and put the vinyl on the turntable.

After a brief and achingly innocent *a capella* version of *The Right Somebody to Love*, the exquisite softness of *Safe in My Garden* welled up.

Dorothy held up the album sleeve. "You ever heard this?"

"No."

"Nice album," she noted as she nodded approvingly at the back cover and slowly swayed with the music.

God, I loved her so. How could she not know? She circled around me and coaxed me up to dance. I didn't hesitate. I was plenty awkward. Stiff as a board. She pulled me close in the most tender way.

"It's okay, Tim," she whispered gently in my ear.

She attempted to lead me, but it was tough going. I kept thinking I should tell her about Darrell, but in a crazy kind of way, I wanted these last moments to be all mine.

"Relax, honey. You're doin' fine." she said.

I leaned in and kissed her, a bold move. She pulled back slightly and smiled, "Timothy." I loved hearing her say my name. The context didn't matter.

I blushed and answered "Dorothy" in return.

She kissed me back.

For me, the world stopped turning when our mouths met. The kiss was hot, sweltering, and oozed sex even though I had no idea what that was. But somehow I knew exactly what it meant.

We stopped dancing. Her big brown eyes invited me in. I was speechless. Captured. Her prisoner forever if that was her wish.

Was the music still playing?

I couldn't tell. It was as if I had giant seashells against my ears.

"If anyone asks," she said, "this was your idea."

She broke our embrace, took my hand, and led me down the hallway to her bedroom. The bed was the only piece of furniture left in the room. There were no blankets, but there were pillows and sheets.

She shut the door behind us. The air was still. Without ceremony, Dorothy peeled her clothes off. The hint to me was that I was supposed to be peeling my things off at the same time. But I was mesmerized watching her remove her clothes. I had never seen nudity in person except my mother's when she stumbled around half-drunk with her house coat hanging open.

But this wasn't some old mom or a native in National Geographic. Dorothy was beautiful. Like the girls in *Playboy*.

She giggled and slipped under the top sheet. All at once, I got a grip on myself and quickly shed my clothes. As I went to enter the bed on my side, she marveled at my erection.

There was a moment where I hovered. Unsure. Dorothy pulled me close.

Her skin was flawless. Soft. Firm. And she smelled like... life.

She didn't just hold me close. She enveloped me.

It was that easy.

And that beautiful.

That memorable.

I was not used to kindness like this.

I helped her get her stereo into the trunk of her car. I was helping her move and I was still denying in my head she was leaving.

She hugged me. Caressed my face. "Oh, Tim."

Her eyes misted over and she kissed me intimately as if I were a lover. And I guess technically I was. But I never wanted to be just one of her lovers, I wanted to be the only one.

"Don't forget. I'm going to come find you when I'm 21," I said with a quiver in my voice.

She shook her head wistfully and said, "Oh, Tim. You're going to meet so many people."

She squeezed my hands, got in her car and started it up. It didn't occur to me to say goodbye. I didn't say anything at all.

Dorothy backed out of the driveway and paused. She blew a kiss and waved before flooring the accelerator.

It was the last time I would ever see her.

I just didn't know it yet.

Warm

On Saturday, I did some shoplifting for gifting purposes. I lurked in front of the magazine rack at *LaVerdiere's* until I thought no one was looking. The new *Playboy* went under my jacket, no sweat. I walked with purpose past the cashier and straight out the door.

Nobody messed with me.

Maybe it was a look on my face.

The next morning, I sandwiched the *Playboy* into a thick Sunday paper and went to the hospital with my armload of deliveries. I did my duty and hung out with the old terminal people.

I was between visits when I caught sight of Darrell's dad. He came out of a room near the end of the hall and drifted to the far end of the corridor to round the corner.

I snuck into Darrell's room. He was in there by himself. He was especially enormous laid out on his back. And the side I saw as I went in—his left side—was banged up, completely encased in casts and bandages. There were IVs in both arms and tubes up his nose and down his throat.

I made my way around the bed so I could see the side of him that was exposed. He was breathing faintly, but otherwise he was gone to the world. "Hey, Elvis," I said into his un-bandaged ear. "I brought you somethin'."

I unfolded the newspaper and held up my stolen treasure. "*Playboy*. It's a big one. More photos than ever."

His eyes were swollen. Blackened. They didn't open.

I gently nudged him. Elvis registered nothing.

I decided to leave the magazine for him to discover later. It was a struggle and a half to lift the edge of Elvis's mattress, but I managed. I slid the *Playboy* underneath and lowered everything back into place, being careful to straighten out the bedding.

I got up to his good ear again. "It's right here under your mattress. Not even looked at or nothin'."

I stood up and put a hand on his shoulder. "What'd they do to you, man?"

No response.

"Elvis, just give me a sign if it was them. Anything."

Not even a finger twitch. He was dead to the world.

I stole back to the doorway and looked back at my comatose friend.

It was the last time I'd ever see him.

That night in my room, I stayed up all night thumbing through my small collection of *Famous Monsters of Filmland*—re-reading every article I'd already read more times than I could remember. I made a wish out loud to God. I wished that Elvis would get better so we could go to California together. We could visit the Ackermansion. Maybe meet Forrest J Ackerman.

I wished for this fantasy with all my might.

I wished my friend love.

Whether he knew it or not.

At the bus stop the next morning, Moosie made it a point of seeking me out. He weaved his way through little kids he pushed out of the way.

"Hey, Illya," he grinned.

"What do you want?" I asked, staring straight ahead.

He giggled. "I heard your friend's dead."

"No, he isn't, 'cause I just talked to him yesterday."

"When was that?" Moosie wanted to know.

"Yesterday." Did I stutter?

Moosie played with me. "In the daytime?"

"Yeah," I declared defiantly.

Moosie feigned sympathy. "Oh. Well, this happened last night." He laughed and coughed at the same time. "Yeah, porky's gone. Just thought you'd want to know."

The bus drove up and squealed to a stop.

Moosie put a foot on the first step and turned to bead on me. "So I guess we have a date for after school?"

I ran. Bolted. I didn't care where I ended up, but I was desperate to escape the bus stop and Moosie and the trailer court and Dorothy who wasn't there anymore.

Moosie yelled after me. "Go ahead and run, pussy! We'll get your bony ass, don't worry!"

After the bus lumbered off, I realized I had nowhere to run. I doubled back to *Sunshine Acres* and grabbed my bike from underneath our trailer.

I pedaled faster than I ever had in my whole life. I rode straight to the hospital and threw the Wonder Bike down on their front lawn. I bulleted down hallways with people calling after me, but I didn't stop until I got to Elvis's room.

His bed was made up.

Ready for someone else.

I was hell on wheels making my way back to the trailer park. I skidded to a stop at Elvis's place and ditched my bike to the ground all in one motion. The construction pick-up was parked in the driveway. As I rushed up to knock, Elvis's old man came out the door and almost collided with me.

I fell back, collected myself, caught my breath. "Somebody told me Darrell is dead."

His stoic dad eyed me up and down, but didn't offer any information.

I was getting nothing off this guy. What the hell. "Well? Is he?" I demanded.

The old man fired up a cigarette, exhaled, and shook his head no.

I was shaking. "He's not at the hospital. Where is he?"

He puffed and stared off to one side. "He's been transferred. We're movin', son. Movin' down south where his grandmother can take care of him."

He tipped his head slightly to me and went inside without looking back. And that was that. In those days, there was generally no discussion between adults and kids. In his mind, he'd done right by me.

You were constantly given half-assed information and expected to move on.

The next week, Elvis's trailer was hauled away. I went over on my bike and sat overseeing the empty lot until dark.

I'd always been without roots. Mobile home dwellers are transient in nature, so I never thought to ask for a forwarding address when I'd spoken with Darrell's dad.

Occasionally, I went over to Dorothy's old trailer and peeked in. It wasn't locked—I guess because there wasn't anything inside to steal. I'd slip inside and sit cross-legged in the middle of the living room floor.

I wanted to be someplace I'd been warm.

I'd fallen asleep in Dorothy's abandoned living room and woke to the sounds of slamming doors and raised voices outside. It was dark out, accentuated by an aberration. Flashing lights brought me to a sitting position.

I spied through the blinds. There was a police car in my driveway. Bill's Cadillac was there. My mother stood on our trailer steps wrapped in a bathrobe. A small crowd of onlookers had gathered.

A police officer held back a middle-aged woman I didn't recognize. She cursed at our trailer and at my mother directly. "I know you're in there, you sonofabitch! You cheating sonofabitch! Come out! Come out and face me!"

Bill appeared in the doorway behind my mother. The cursing woman strained so hard to lunge at him, her clothes tore away from the officer's grasp. A second officer sprang into action to pull her back. She kicked and screamed. The cops were pissed off. They wedged her into the back of the squad car and forced the door shut. She slapped her palms in a frenzy against the glass.

Bill called out to the cops, "She's crazy. What can I tell you?"

The officers shook their heads in agreement and apologized for the intrusion before getting into their patrol car and leaving.

Releasing the blinds, I leaned back against the wall and slid down to the floor. I extended my legs and cupped my hands over my head.

I stared across the empty living room and let my eyes adjust. I heard Bill's Cadillac start up. I peeked out the blinds and watched him back up and out.

I left Dorothy's place and went over to my own trailer. The door was locked. I used my key to let myself in.

My mother scurried out of her bedroom. "Who's there?"

"It's just me."

"Who's there?" she repeated stridently.

"It's just *me*."

She squinted and finally recognized me. She was disappointed. She headed back into her room and muttered over her shoulder, "Where have you been?"

"None of your business," I informed her on my way past her to my room.

She popped her head into the hallway. "What did you just say to me?"

"Nothing." I meant to slam my door, but stopped short of making a statement when it caught on a sweater I'd left balled up on the floor. I kicked the sweater out of the way and pushed the door shut. I made sure to click the lock.

Just in time. She was on the other side. "What did you just say to me?"

Jesus Christ. "Nothing."

She tried the handle. "Open this door."

"No." I slipped off my shoes and fell back on my bed.

She banged a fist against the veneer on the other side. "Open this door!"

"Why don't you call the cops?" Now I was just being funny.

I heard her shuffle off to her bedroom.

I chuckled and talked out loud to myself. "Yeah, mother. Why don't you call the cops on your disobedient son? They should get here pretty quickly on account of they already know the way."

It was one of many nights I would lie awake on my bed.

Everything I cared about was gone.

I hated my life.

Illya Kuryakin

It was my 3rd morning without a bodyguard at the bus stop. I had a stack of hardcover books I'd checked out from the library in my arms.

I was not itching for confrontation. Truth be told, I was sick to my stomach. I hadn't been there 30 seconds before Moosie and his dimwits blustered over.

Moosie smacked his right fist into his left palm a couple of times. "Hey, peckerhead, where'd you take off to the other day? To cry or somethin'?"

I ignored him.

"Hey, Illya," he persisted. "Look at me."

I refused to acknowledge his shit.

Moosie circled around and when he was out of my peripheral vision, he cuffed my right ear. I didn't see it coming and it knocked me off balance. It hurt like a motherfucker. I righted myself.

"Cut it out," I deadpanned.

Moosie snaked around in front of me. "Cut it out? You're Illya Kuryakin—why don't you just Karate chop me?"

Richard's eyes lit up and he moved into my space. "Oh, you watch *The Man from U.N.C.L.E.*, too, huh?"

I was willing to grasp at any tether of connection. "You watch it?" I asked hopefully. Dammit. I knew better. I should have kept my mouth shut.

"No," he answered passively.

Elwood came around Richard's side to form a human stupid wall. "That's a show for homos. It's all made up."

God, Elwood was such a low-flying imbecile.

"Yeah, no kidding," I wise-cracked.

Richard shoved me sideways. I kept a poker face. I didn't want to provoke higher levels of abuse. He shoved me again and this time I saw it coming, so I was able to stand strong. My resistance egged him on.

He faked a punch my way and I dodged to one side.

"Yeah, you ain't so tough without chubby, are you?" he leered.

Moosie snapped his fingers to get Richard's attention. "I told you that fat fuck was dead, didn't I?"

My entire body tensed. "He's not dead, you little mouse."

There were a lot of things I could have called him, but calling him a mouse really set him off. Moosie practically had smoke coming out his ears.

He took a step toward me.

"What did you just call me, you little welfare beggar?"

I'll give him one thing—he was good at name calling and no matter how monotonously he called shit out, it always stung a little. For some unexplained reason, I laughed. In his face. Derisively. I couldn't believe I was purposely jacking his ass up.

He couldn't believe it either. A black cloud massed over his head and he thrashed my books out of my arms. His boneheads guffawed when my shit fanned out, clattering to the ground. It was so unnecessary. So idiotic and infantile. Such a broken record.

"Did you just call me a mouse?"

I didn't care anymore. I was willing to take a beating in exchange for being able to tell this clown to fuck off. I puffed up. Ready to talk back.

He challenged me again, only peppered with more anger. "You call me a mouse?"

"Yeah, Moosie. Or should I say *Mous*ie.?" Go ahead. Beat on me. I didn't care.

Apparently, I was playing right into scenarios running through their underdeveloped minds.

I knelt down on one knee to collect my books and papers. Elwood kicked them away.

As I got to my feet, Moosie hauled off and kicked me square in the ass, knocking me to the ground. He'd clipped the end of my tailbone. It hummed. I knew I was injured. There was no end to what a prick this little bastard was.

"C'mon, pussy. Get up. I dare ya," Moosie threatened.

Either I was a man or I wasn't. It was that simple. I rose slowly with intent and attitude.

Elwood spit on the ground. "I wouldn'ta got back up. What are you, stupid?"

"No, he's Illya Kuryakin," Moosie cracked.

They all had a laugh at my expense and then Moosie gave the nod.

Elwood and Richard each grabbed one of my arms. God, how many times did I have to go through this shit with these mouth-breathers?

For a second, I panicked. Then I did something absolutely ludicrous in retrospect. My whole being came into play. I wiggled free and broke away. My adrenaline surge spooked them.

I went into a Karate combat stance.

Without hesitation, Moosie's two big goofs backed off. They were trying to figure out how to act when a predictable victim becomes unpredictable. It was a new experience for them.

Moosie's face contorted with rage at his posse of pussies. "What are you scared of?" he yelled.

Moosie made a move and rushed me. Instinctively, I stuck out my right arm, ramrod stiff. It caught him right in his Adam's apple and he went down like I'd beaned him between the eyes with a fastball. It was a fluke. I'd played defense and he ran into my wall.

It could have killed him. Moosie was unable to speak. Or breathe much, for that matter. He grabbed at his throat. I got nervous, but I must admit, it was a great effect.

He pointed to Richard and Elwood and motioned them toward me.

Richard and Elwood encircled me in a half-assed kind of way, but they were bright enough to keep a safe distance. I was on fire. I didn't care if I took a beating or not. I was through making it easy for them. Richard faced off with me while Elwood edged around to my rear.

"Get him!" Moosie rasped.

Richard charged me. It felt like it all went by in slow motion. He closed in and leapt through the air for a tackle, but I ducked protectively and hunched over with my knees bent, cringing before the impact.

Thank God for happy accidents. Richard hit me perfectly and went flying across my bent over back right as I stood up, making it look like I'd intentionally flipped him over me. Richard bowled into Elwood and they both went down.

I marveled at fate. And I was smart enough and quick enough to capitalize on this divine intervention.

I popped back into combat stance.

Richard and Elwood clawed over each other to escape.

Elwood led the way exclaiming "That fucker knows Judo, man!"

I brought my full attention to Moosie who didn't know what to think. I held my right arm up over my head in a threatening mock Karate chop.

Moosie threw up a palm to protect himself.

You little fuck. I should kill you, I thought. I faked a punch and he flinched. "Two for flinching, Moosie."

I punched his left bicep. Twice. Hard. He couldn't get any sounds out. I grabbed him and wrangled him to the ground. I was pissed and in control. "Pick up my books and clean 'em off," I demanded.

Moosie quaked in my presence and did as he was told.

And that was it.

I had the balls lying around.

I just needed to strap them on.

I walked into our trailer and it looked sterile. The furniture was there, but all personal touches were absent. My mother came out of her room manhandling two large suitcases that had seen better days. One had long stretches of tape securing it shut. The other had a handle fashioned out of multiple cords of clothesline.

Butter on your shoes anyone?

She dumped the suitcases with a thud near the door and hunched over to catch her breath. "We're leaving," she wheezed out.

Wow. Another unannounced move under cover.

"Where are we going?"

"To live with Bill."

"What'll happen to our trailer?"

"I'm selling it."

"But Bill's married."

"His wife moved out."

"You just met him practically. And what about your job?"

"I already quit."

I stared at her. Hard. Eyes burning.

Well, at least I wouldn't have to see Moosie anymore.

The old bag was good for something once in a while.

Full Circle

I hadn't been back to Glen Cove in 41 years. I'd driven up from Virginia and stopped off on my way to visit my half-sister in Fort Kent. It was wintertime. Cold, windy. The layout seemed smaller. Foreign.

I cruised Steve Oreno's. Not there anymore. Nor was he in the phone listings.

I sat in my olive green Audi sedan staring at an indelible part of my fabric. Our old haunt was an abandoned weather-beaten shell.

I got out of my car and walked with my coat open. Loose gravel bits in the unkempt driveway surrendered under my feet. Standing at the base of the 3 rickety wooden steps leading up to the small porch, I saw the notices taped up in the window of the front door. Scheduled to be torn down. Even though I knew there wouldn't be anything to see, I tested my way up the steps and peeked in.

Lifeless random clutter shrouded in a heavy blanket of dirt and dust.

I tried the door handle. Locked.

Oh, well.

I half-jumped off the porch and got back in my car.

The trailer court across the street was still there, but worse for the wear. The *Sunshine Acres* sign was gone, replaced by a $2 orange letters on black background sign reading PRIVATE PROPERTY.

I parked inside the front entrance and traced where Elvis and I had spent so much time together.

Two kids—one tall and skinny, the other short and squat—zipped past me on bikes. They went around on either side, almost clipping my arms.

"Hey, dildo!" yelled Skinny.

Squat boy chimed in. "Watch where you're goin', loser!"

I had to laugh as they curved off behind a trailer and disappeared.

I needed gas on my way out and I stopped at a mom and pop place. After I filled my tank, I went inside to pay because the pump was ancient, and didn't take credit cards. I handed cash to the short greasy guy in oil-stained overalls on the other side of the counter. As he rang up the sale, I caught a glimpse of his nametag.

MOOSIE

I'd always wondered how he'd ended up. Whether he'd stayed mean. And here he was. Pot-bellied and bald.

He handed back my change and a receipt.

"Thanks for comin' in," he said on automatic pilot. "Come again."

I counted my change. It wasn't right.

I held out my hand. "I think you still owe me two cents."

Moosie got a funny look on his face, but he didn't question me. He reached into the drawer and handed over two pennies.

"Oh, sorry."

I smiled.

He didn't seem mean anymore.

Just bored and stupid.

What's True

I did a lot of thinking as I cruised away in my Audi. They say it's not good to live in the past, but I think it's okay to splash around in your memories from time to time. I find it helpful, even healthy, but I don't swim in it.

The individuals I met in 1969 were important in their time and context. The people and events that introduced themselves in my later life dwarfed my experiences as a teenager.

I thought about my mother and Bill. After stirring up trouble in a number of unsuspecting lives, they got married. Their doomed union lasted through most of my high school years. They both became worse drunks. Bill beat my mother repeatedly, and me as well, until he committed suicide one morning after I left for school.

My mother lived until she was 83. She never stopped drinking. In fact, she spent the last three decades of her life drinking herself to a slow death in front of a constantly blaring TV. All of this was financed with welfare and social security checks.

In her later years, my mother drank plastic bottle vodka exclusively. Her ritual began each morning at 5:30 AM with a water glass full. She kept her booze in the freezer so she wouldn't have to clutter up space in the glass with ice. Sometimes she added reduced-acid orange juice for coloring. In the last 10 years of her life, she laughed during the first hour of the *Today* show, was blotto by mid-morning, and passed out in her chair by noon. She'd wake up a couple of hours later to catch up on soaps and begin round 2. I knew better than to call her in the afternoon or evening because she wouldn't remember talking to me. As she got older, her nights were over by 7:30 PM.

Her weekly diet of alcohol, cake, ice cream, sweets, and an occasional roast beef sandwich managed to sustain her. She used Alka-Seltzer twice a day, ate Tums like they were mints, and drank Pepto-Bismol straight out of the bottle. The abuse she inflicted on herself would have killed a normal person.

Amazingly enough, it wasn't cirrhosis of the liver that did her in. It was kidney failure. She could have lived even longer if she'd wanted to follow the advice of physicians who examined her, but that was not her way. Every so often, she blacked out and had to be rushed to the hospital emergency room. On each of these excursions, she checked herself out the very next day before the doctors could follow up.

If a doctor managed to get a counseling in during an examination, the advice was always "You need to stop drinking if you want to survive" and her answer was always that she had no intention of abstaining. She refused free dialysis and medical assistance. She always claimed that since

246

she'd been a nurse, she knew what really went on in hospitals. She knew more than the doctors did.

I made a number of attempts to get my mother on the right track. But she was stubborn, selfish, and spiteful right up until her exit.

My mother's journey was not an easy one and I came to some level of understanding and compassion about that. I came to a realization that she arrived on the scene without all the tools. However, that did little to temper my experience with her. The part I couldn't get past was her vice-like unwillingness to stop hurting herself and those around her. There were numerous times she became so destructive, I refused to communicate with her. Sometimes for years at a stretch.

Her example was double-edged. The upside was that I made it a point as an adult to not go down a lot of dark roads she'd traveled. The downside was that I manifested some of her bad qualities despite my best efforts. The upside to the downside is I got better as I went along, rather than worse. The legacy of alcoholism she left behind did not always serve me well. But even at my worst, I was functional. I never had to have a bucket beside my chair and I never made my kids clean up after me.

I wish I'd had a mother. A real mother. Someone to guide me and provide encouragement. Someone who loved me enough to make the sacrifices a parent is supposed to make. Anyone who tells you those things don't matter is a liar. If you've got parents who really love and care for you, you're one of the lucky ones.

To me, the older my mother got, the more she became an enigma. A complete stranger. As a younger man, I was desperate to make some connection, but I could never crack the code. As an older man, I lost interest in deciphering someone I would cross the street to avoid had we not been related.

I sat down with her for a few days a couple of years before she died. It'd been a decade since I'd seen her and I was shocked by her diminished appearance. This was the person who had terrorized my childhood and held it for ransom. I could have literally reached down and crushed her with a thumb. And in that moment, I wasn't angry anymore. I just had this tremendous sense of loss. Of what had not been accomplished.

Rather than investigating introspection in her last days, she became meaner.

I had a chance to go to her bedside during her final hours and I politely refused.

She died in a drug-induced coma.

I don't miss her.

I looked Darrell up on the internet, and through a series of phone calls, I discovered he'd died a decade earlier—complications from diabetes. Sometimes I think I'm better off without the technology. It would have been nicer to imagine he was still out there somewhere.

The real Elvis died at the age of 42 in August of 1977. I was getting ready for work. The radio was on in the living room and they played Elvis songs back to back. After a few numbers, a DJ got on and spoke about Elvis dying. I felt hollow that day.

I never did try and find Dorothy when I turned 21 like I swore I would. She was right. I just didn't want her to be at the time. I hope she found happiness and someone to take care of her like I did. In a way, I think I was in love with her, in as much as I could understand what love was at that age. I never looked at what happened between us as something dirty or illicit. I never got the impression I was being taken advantage of. I was really lucky that my first experience with sex was a great one.

I thought about Gene. How old was he now? Early 40s? What was his upbringing like? Did he end up with stepfathers and were they kind or cruel to him? What was his relationship with his mother like? How much did he know about her?

I wondered what had happened to Steve Oreno. Not finding him in person or in the phone book crushed me a little.

In May of 2000, I ran into Forrest J Ackerman in a chance meeting where he surprised me by offering an invitation to the Ackermansion the following Saturday. I shouldn't have been surprised because Forrey invited *everyone* to the Ackermansion on weekends he was in town.

I waited with about 25 other fans, and at the appointed time, his car pulled up. When he stepped out of his sedan, it was a surreal fantasy moment for all of us. On that sunny California afternoon in Los Feliz, the sun had risen in our minds.

He unlocked the gate to his mini-mansion and led us through room after room, each stacked floor to ceiling with countless jumbled pieces of monster and sci-fi memorabilia in varying stages of decay. The place had seen better days. And yet it was magnificent.

Forrest was old. Somewhat frail. He sat in an easy chair in his living room and let us roam freely.

I had a full circle moment where I was able to speak with him. One-on-one. And I don't think the full import of those precious minutes really found a nest in my mind until I typed this sentence.

This was someone I'd dreamt about meeting one day. And I was living it. We talked for all of 15 minutes. But it was *my* 15 minutes.

He mentioned his wife who'd died a decade earlier from wounds sustained in a random attack on the streets of Italy. It overwhelmed him to speak of it.

He confided a magazine dealer once told him his monster periodicals held the honor of being the most shoplifted magazine on the stands. I neglected to tell him I was guilty on multiple accounts.

After more wandering through his mansion, I asked him to autograph some *Famous Monsters* items which he did gladly, as if he was flattered to be asked. He posed for pictures and told corny jokes. He really was this sweet soul— a grandfather to so many lost boys in the world. Unique and irreplaceable.

I only wish I could have shared that splinter of time with Darrell.

Forrest J Ackerman passed away in December of 2008. He was 92 years old. Of the countless thousands of artifacts he'd collected over the years, he was left with a mere one hundred of his favorites. He'd sold everything else to pay for litigation over the rights to *Famous Monsters of Filmland*.

I'm happy I got to meet him while he was still surrounded by his treasure trove of collectibles. It was a privilege to be welcomed into the inner sanctum and put my arm around an idol that made a difference to a lot of people.

I spent a lot of time in misdirected anger, much like the bullies who tortured me. I see now the only difference between us was in how we manifested our internal fires. I had to come to an agreement with anger. I had to stop wallowing in it. In my youth, anger was often the only survival mechanism I had at my disposal. So liberating myself was a struggle. I bit a lot of hands that tried to feed me along the way.

I had to find a place in my heart to trust and even when I'd managed to carve out that space, I fought commitment. After using my massive insecurities as weapons to destroy countless bonds, I was fortunate to meet and marry my soul mate—a person who managed to find and cultivate what was good in me. I fought her on character development. Many times. To her credit, she saw something I couldn't see in myself and refused to give up. If enough love pours into your life, you'll crack. But you gotta be willing to let it in. It's a strange feeling when you're not used to it.

We tried to nurture our children in ways we were not. From an early age, we instilled that much was expected. We impressed on our kids that sharing your humanity and talents makes you and the world a better place. We tried to give them some guidelines so they'd have a solid foundation to build their lives on.

If time travel was possible, I wonder if I'd want to reach back and have a heart-to-heart with my 14-year-old self. Maybe. Maybe not. Maybe it's better if everything's discovered organically.

But if I could have told myself just one truth, it would've been this. You're not alone.

It gets better.

Trust me on this one thing.

You're going to meet so many people.

About the Author

Doug Bari is an award-winning actor, writer, director, and filmmaker. This is his first book.

Made in the USA
Middletown, DE
17 June 2018